MURDER
OFF
ROUTE 82

— AN EVE SAWYER MYSTERY —

MURDER
OFF
ROUTE 82

— AN EVE SAWYER MYSTERY —

JANE SUEN

Murder off Route 82: An Eve Sawyer Mystery

Jane Suen books are available for order through Ingram Press Catalogues.

www.janesuen.com

Printed in the United States of America

First Printing: December 2021

Library of Congress Control Number: 2021923290

Ebook ISBN: 978-1-951002-17-6

Paperback ISBN: 978-1-951002-18-3

Audiobook ISBN: 978-1-951002-20-6

To my loyal readers, whose support means the world to me.

To those who have suffered the loss or disappearance of a loved one.

To the memory of Laura Furuta.

Finally, to Tim B, who said this about snakes:
"I love them, have since I was a kid."

PROLOGUE

She had gone to meet him, and she was early—the first to appear.

The cool, crisp air caressed her cheeks, sweeping away the unrelenting heat waves of summer. The lush, green foliage had faded and surrendered to the changing season. The leaves swirled, dancing in the wind, their glorious fall colors a kaleidoscope of changing patterns.

The crunch of leaves under firm footsteps announced his arrival. She waited, plucking a fallen, rusty-red leaf from her hair and releasing it.

Her body went numb when he said it, delivering those words: "I'm sorry." He turned his back and slipped away, retreating before the tears trickled down her cheeks. She held back the sob caught in the back of her throat and stared down at her hands, whispering his name.

CHAPTER ONE

THE FAMILIAR SIGHT CAME INTO VIEW. I WAS WELCOMED back to campus by distinguished-looking brick academic buildings designed in the glory of ancient architecture. They were complimented perfectly by expansive, grassy lawns, cultivated flower beds, and the fluttering flag atop an enormous flagpole in the center of a circular drive.

As much as I had enjoyed the summer and the time I spent with Cassie and Bob at her grandmother's Lolly Beach cottage, I was excited to be back. The vibrant pulse at the start of the new school year at Midway College was palpable. The chatter and bursts of laughter as students greeted one another on their way to and from classes, crowded into the bookstore, milled about at the student center, or sprawled out on the grass or on benches were all exhilarating.

I sported a wide grin. It was great to be back. I had signed up for another class with Professor Reynolds in the journalism department.

I made my way to the campus store to pick up some new pencils and a few other school supplies.

"Eve!"

I recognized that voice, rich, deep, and warm. I spotted the lanky build and watched as Bob Harding strode toward me where I stood at the end of the checkout line, his long legs picking up the pace. His unruly, full head of hair framed his smiling, suntanned face.

"Well, look at you!" I said, grinning from ear to ear. Bob, Cassie, and I were lab partners in chemistry last semester. Cassie had invited us to her beach house, and it turned out to be more than a vacation. Who would have thought there'd be a murder to solve at the idyllic beach? And with everything that had happened, I'd gotten to know Bob better. After I left, Cassie decided to stay there and take a leave of absence from school this fall semester. I missed her already.

"You ready for class?" he asked.

"Pretty much, now that I've stocked up on my supply of trusty pencils."

"Are you taking Professor Reynolds' class?"

"Yup, signed up for that."

Bob set down his items, all the while talking to me as the cashier finished checking me out. I turned to wait for him. Bob was so organized; I would've thought he had gotten everything already. He looked at me sheepishly as if he'd read my mind.

"Extras, in case," he said as the cashier stuffed a couple of items in his bag.

We walked outside, pausing on the edge of the sidewalk to make room for the brisk foot traffic. I didn't want to leave, not yet. For a moment we stood, comfortable in each other's silence. I basked in the gentle warmth of the sun on my face and sucked in the clean air, smelling of earthy, fresh-cut grass. Somewhere in the distance, squeals and laughter erupted, adding to the noise around us.

A student jostled me as he rushed by, reminding me to check the time. I glanced at my cell. "I've got to run," I said, making a quick mental calculation of the distance to my next class and how fast I could sprint. "Catch you later?"

Bob smiled and nodded.

&.

THE DAY SPED BY, images of new faces mixed in with sounds of easy and harder-to-pronounce names. The list of reading materials and homework was piling up quickly. I was ready to hit the ground running. I could already tell which classes I liked. I had to take one more prerequisite before I graduated, and with the rest, I had some choice.

As the end of the day approached, my mind started to wander. I had written notes on what I had to do to be organized. Before I plunged into my homework, I took a walk around campus. I loved this time of the year when the leaves turned to yellow, orange, red, and shades in between. It seemed to be nature's last hurrah before the icy breath of winter casts a deathly spell over the land. I walked down the well-worn path around the circular arc in front of the campus before heading back toward the journalism building, the bookstore, and the student center that made up the hub of student activity.

I liked school. It didn't come easy for me. I worked hard for my grades and made the dean's list again last semester. Mom was proud of me. I lived about an hour and a half away, which was close enough to go home on weekends when I could get away, but far enough that I could maintain my independence. It was a deal I made with my mom. She respected it and trusted me to do my own thing even if it meant I'd be left to make my own mistakes. She realized from early on that I was an old soul. I was pretty level-headed, and I liked to make my own decisions. And with my good grades and scholarships, I'd been able to pay my own way through college, supplemented with part-time work, grants, and loans.

I was excitedly looking forward to this semester.

CHAPTER TWO

THE FIRST FEW WEEKS OF SCHOOL FLEW BY. I DOVE INTO my studies and school activities, and I renewed friendships while juggling a crazy schedule. I barely had time for myself. I had a pretty good load, and it kept me busy. I drove myself hard during the week, but by the time weekends arrived, I welcomed them and let up a bit. They were a chance to catch up on my sleep and provided a bit of "me time" before the next week.

It was a Saturday morning when I got the call. I was still in my PJs and in bed. Groggy, my eyelids fluttered, raising to a slit, then down again. My mind commanded the insistent ringing to go away as I hugged the pillow to my head. It robbed me of a sweet dream as I'd slept, curled in a comfy position. Cursing, I finally snatched my phone off the nightstand to see that I had a missed call earlier from the same number.

"Hello," I mumbled, stifling a yawn. Nobody should expect me to be cheery this early in the morning—on a Saturday, no less.

"Eve?"

I paused, my half-awake brain fumbling and searching for a face to go with the voice.

"This is Mrs. Landon. Sallie Rae's mom."

Why was her mom calling me ... and at this hour? I knew Sallie Rae, but we weren't exactly close friends. I'd met her at a party last year. With a name like Sallie Rae, it was kind of hard to forget her—a tumble of soft blond curls framing a heart-shaped, pretty face, like sunshine and sweetness and innocence. And when she spoke, the words dribbled out of her lips like honey.

"I'm sorry. Did I wake you?" Mrs. Landon asked.

"Uh no, it's all right." I didn't want to hurt her feelings. Rubbing my heavy-lidded eyes, I forced a laugh. I was deprived of sleep and cranky, having stayed up too late last night. And I hadn't had my coffee yet.

"What's up, Mrs. Landon?"

"Sallie Rae hasn't called since Thursday morning. She was supposed to come home for the weekend and ... well ... she didn't show up."

"Have you talked to her roommate?"

"Erika said she hasn't seen Sallie Rae since yesterday. She went to bed early and didn't see Sallie Rae come home last night. When I called this morning, Erika checked and said she wasn't there."

"Would she know if Sallie Rae had come in and left again?"

"I asked her the same question. Erika said she couldn't be sure, but the room looked like it hadn't been disturbed last night."

"Have you tried calling Sallie Rae?"

"Yes, I've called and left voicemails and texts."

"No answers?"

A sob on the other end.

"I'm worried," she said. Then there was unmistakable sniffling.

"Take a deep breath. Take several, nice and slow," I said, doing my best to calm her.

"Sallie Rae told me about you ... solving cases at Murder Creek and Lolly Beach." She paused as if she was taking a drag on a cigarette and exhaling. "Can you help me ... *please?*" Maybe she wasn't used to begging, but there was no mistaking the urgent pleading in her voice.

"I'm a journalism student," I said. I hated to promise her and not be able to deliver.

After I met Sallie Rae, we'd seen each other occasionally. She was better at keeping in touch than I was, and I heard from her over the summer when she went home to work. She was close to her mom, a single parent, so the fact that she'd told her about me came as no surprise. I had downplayed what I did on those cases to Sallie Rae, but she may have exaggerated.

"She's a good girl, my Sallie Rae," her mother said as her voice cracked.

"When was the last time you talked to her?"

"Thursday. Briefly. It was between classes, and she was going to call me back yesterday and let me know for sure about coming home this weekend."

"How did she sound?"

"I couldn't tell. There were a lot of noises in the background."

"Was she upset? Did she mention anything else?"

"It was a quick call." Mrs. Landon sighed, the weary kind of sigh. "Sallie Rae is my only child, and we've always had a tight bond. Although this time, she ended it abruptly."

"What do you mean?" I asked.

"It wasn't like our usual calls, where I'd say 'I love you' and she'd say 'I love you' back." She paused. "This time, I felt there might have been something wrong."

CHAPTER THREE

I WAS WIDE AWAKE NOW, MY SENSES ON ALERT, PICKING up ringing alarm bells.

"Have you contacted the authorities?"

"The sheriff's office here."

"You'll need to notify the Midway College police— we don't know for sure when, or if, Sallie Rae left campus. You have the number?"

"I've got the main number. I'll call in and report her missing."

"Would you like me to check around here?" I blurted out.

"Yes, please. You know some of her friends?"

"Yes." I threw my legs over and jumped out of bed. "Let me see what I can find out. I'll get back to you."

I got dressed, pulled on one of my favorite T-shirts and a pair of comfortable jeans, brushed my teeth, and pulled my hair into a ponytail. I quickly brewed coffee in my small coffeemaker and poured it in a travel cup to go, snatching a cranberry scone on my way out.

❧

SALLIE RAE SHARED a house for students close to the campus. It was like one of many in the area surrounding Midway College, painted a dreary color, bland, cookie-cutter style. Those houses were always in demand, the annual contracts signed before the end of the school year. The owners did minimal fix-ups, painting, and quick touch-ups between renters. As long as the renters lined up and there was a wait-list, the owners didn't make extensive renovations. I knew Sallie Rae didn't seem to mind, and she had snatched up this rental as soon as it became available. Word of mouth and a stroke of good luck got her a spot. She moved in with a roommate, Erika.

I drove to her place. The car parked in the driveway wasn't Sallie Rae's minicar.

"Hi, Erika," I said as the door opened. I didn't have to wait after I knocked. She was expecting me.

"Come on in," Erika said. She held the door open. "Sallie Rae's mom said you'd be coming by."

My lips curled up in a half-smile. I stepped into the house and looked around the small living room and the kitchen.

"Her bedroom is down the hallway, last door," she said.

I glanced in the direction of Sallie Rae's slightly ajar bedroom door. "This the way she left it?"

"Yes."

"And you haven't seen her since yesterday morning?"

Erika shook her head. "Nope. I'd gotten up earlier, and we exchanged a few quick words before I rushed out for my first class."

I stopped in front of Sallie Rae's door and peeked into her room. Erika was breathing down my neck. Bright sunlight streamed into the room, passing through the slats of the blinds. Sneakers lay past the doorway where they had been tossed, bunched-up socks thrown on top.

My fingers trembled as I tapped the wooden panel and eased the door open slowly. It was messy, all right, with clothes scattered across the room on the furniture and on the floor. I took in the bed, its sheets rumpled. A pastel-blue comforter spilled onto the floor as if someone had stepped out of bed and gotten their foot caught in it and dragged it onto the carpet. I gingerly walked around to the other side, checking to be sure nothing had fallen behind it.

A small desk was pushed against the wall, with a singular lamp and some books. A picture of Sallie Rae and Drew was propped on the end of the desk.

"You know Drew?" Erika said it rhetorically, not expecting an answer to an obvious question.

I'd seen Drew last semester. Sallie Rae had dated him, and they quickly became a twosome. When he took the summer off to travel in Europe, Sallie Rae was crushed and missed him terribly. But she'd already had a job lined up back home, where she could save money and live with her mom, so taking time off to be with him was not an option.

"What about Drew?" I asked. "How's Sallie Rae been acting lately? Did she say anything to you?"

"Well, I think something may have happened between them. Sallie Rae was distraught. Upset. I'd never seen her like that."

"This was when?"

"Wednesday. I came home from class, and she was in her room. When she didn't come out at dinnertime, I knocked on her door. But she didn't want to talk to me."

"When did you last see her?"

"Yesterday morning when we were in the kitchen."

"How did she look?"

"Not her usual self. Her eyes were puffy and red, her voice hoarse." Erika paused, shaking her head. "It was so unlike her. I'd never seen her that way."

That didn't sound like the chirpy Sallie Rae I was acquainted with. "What did she say to you?"

"She didn't say exactly, but I think they had a fight, and Drew broke up with her." Erika paused again, rubbing her neck. "I think she was still in shock and hurting a lot."

"Did she give any details?"

Erika frowned. "Nope, and I didn't pry."

"No clue?"

She shook her head, shrugging her shoulders.

"Know where Drew lives?"

Erika picked up her cell phone and scrolled through her contact list. She reached for a sticky note on Sallie Rae's desk, scribbled on it, and tore off the sheet. "Drew's address and his cell number."

"Great, thank you," I murmured as I rushed out the door.

CHAPTER FOUR

I drove over to Drew's house. It wasn't far. It sat in a row of nondescript student housing, each unit similar to the other. The porch railing was slanted. A beer bottle had rolled among dandelions and weeds, stopping at the edge of the walkway.

The only pieces of furniture on the porch were a small table with empty cans and a full ashtray on it and a sunken, well-worn, stained couch on its last legs. Probably from several tenants ago. The vibe screamed student housing. I ran up the steps and almost expected loud music to be blaring from the inside, but everything was quiet. Too quiet. I knocked on the door, waited, then called out Drew's name. Still no answer.

I retrieved the slip of paper with his number and dialed. When he didn't pick up, I left a voicemail. "Drew, this is Eve, Sallie Rae's friend. Please call me. It's urgent."

This time, I pounded on the door, but no one came,

so I stepped off the porch and made my way to the backyard. Peering in the backdoor window, I could see it opened into the kitchen area. Dirty dishes were stacked in the sink. A solitary mug sat on the counter. Empty grocery bags slouched on the kitchen table, a pile of mail dumped next to them. Drew Walker lived here with his roommate, Randall Quinn, but nobody was in sight.

I called Drew's number and listened for the ringing again. It was louder this time. I jumped at the shrill sound echoing in an otherwise quiet house. He wasn't answering, but his cell phone was there.

I walked back to my car parked across the street, got in, and sat, trying to figure out what to do next. I wasn't prepared to wait all day, and the idea of doing that wasn't appealing. I decided to stay put for now in case Drew showed up soon. Meanwhile, I made a list of some mutual friends of mine and Sallie Rae's to call.

The tunes of a melody burst out on my phone, star- tling me. A streak of guilt ran through me when I real- ized I was supposed to call Bob this morning. Although we hadn't set a specific time, we'd made plans to meet today.

"Hi, Bob," I said.

"What's up with you?"

"Hey, I'm sorry I didn't call," I said, knowing he'd see through me if I made a flimsy excuse. It was better to come right out and apologize.

"That's not like you. What's going on?"

"You remember Sallie Rae?"

"Yeah, I met her a few times."

"Well, her mom called me this morning. She hadn't heard from her in a while. Said Sallie Rae was supposed to go home this weekend. Her roommate said she hadn't seen her since yesterday morning," I blurted out, my words tumbling over each other.

"Where're you now?"

"I'm parked outside Drew's house. I drove here to talk to him, but he isn't home."

"Hold on," Bob said in his soothing, deep, bass voice. "I know Drew's place. Stay there. I'm coming right over to see you. We can talk in person."

"You sure?" I was going to stick it out for a while, so I definitely wouldn't mind having Bob's company.

"I'll grab us some coffee and donuts on the way."

I smiled. "And egg biscuits, please."

It wasn't long before a pickup pulled up behind me. A glance in my rearview mirror confirmed it was Bob in the driver's seat. He got out and approached my car, pulled the handle on the passenger door, and slid in. I caught a whiff of sinfully delicious buttery biscuits and fresh coffee. I perked up immediately. I could eat and not gain a pound. I had no excuses when it came to good food.

"You got those egg biscuits?"

"Yes, ma'am," Bob said, laughing. "I know you don't eat meat."

So considerate. I made a mental note.

"Thank you. What are you having?"

"I got the same thing. Actually, I ordered four of them." He grinned.

"You remembered," I said, laughing. I definitely saw his cheeks flush red.

While we ate, I filled Bob in on the details and admitted to peeking in Drew's house. Bob didn't interrupt me, listening intently until I was finished. He asked a few questions to clear a few things up. At one point, he said, "Stop," leaning over to wipe a sticky crumb hanging precipitously on the edge of my lip.

I took another gulp of my coffee. The box of donuts sat on the back seat. I was beginning to think this stakeout wasn't so bad.

I asked Bob if he had the number for Randall Quinn, who was Drew's roommate. He shook his head but didn't waste any time texting around. I noticed he was as agile using one thumb to type as I was using both thumbs. I pulled out my notepad and wrote down the names of the people we contacted.

The next name on the list was Cindy. I had met her last year at a party. We'd left about the same time and walked together to where our cars were parked. I couldn't start my car. When she saw I was having car trouble, she gave me a jump like it was no big deal. She made it look so easy with her efficiency and smooth motions. Her father had raised her like the boy he didn't have. I'd run into her every now and then, but our paths hadn't crossed a lot—until now. I knew she was friends with Sallie Rae.

"Eve!" Cindy squealed. She'd answered on the first ring.

"I was hoping you'd remember me," I said.

"How could I not?" she teased.

We chatted for a brief moment to catch up before I jumped to the reason for my call.

"What can I do for you?" Cindy was businesslike, and she went straight to the point. I liked this about her.

"I got a call from Sallie Rae's mom. She said Sallie Rae had talked about coming this weekend, but she didn't call or show up last night or this morning. I'm calling around to see what I can find out. Have you seen her lately?"

"I bumped into her in front of the library yesterday."

My ears perked up. "How was she? Did you talk?"

"Only for a few minutes. We don't have any classes together this semester."

"Did she happen to mention Drew?"

"No, but I asked Sallie Rae about him because I knew he'd traveled all over Europe this summer. I'm seriously thinking of doing something like that after I graduate. Take a gap year off before settling down."

"That'd be cool," I said, pausing. "What did she say?"

"She gave me a weird look when I mentioned Drew."

"Did she tell you they broke up?"

"I didn't ask. She was vague, and I didn't press her for details."

"Sallie Rae's mom sounded really worried. Said it wasn't like her to not call or show up. Did you notice anything else when you spoke to her?"

"Well, she said she needed chocolates and mumbled

something about running to the store after class. What do you think happened to her?"

"Don't know. I'm trying to retrace her steps from yesterday."

"I'm afraid I haven't been much help."

"Actually, you have. About what time did you talk to Sallie Rae?"

"Econ ended right before noon. Then I walked to the library. So I'd say around noon."

"Did she mention going home or anything else?"

Cindy paused, before saying, "No, she said she had one more class, psychology, in the afternoon."

"Thanks for your help."

I ended the call. Bob was watching me, his lips twitching.

He was bursting with news the minute my call ended.

"I got a text back from one of the guys." His face betrayed him. His eyebrows raised, and his eyes sparkled.

"Oh yeah? Tell me."

"Drew's car had been sighted."

I sucked in my breath. "Was Sallie Rae with him?"

He shook his head.

"Was he driving?"

"They couldn't tell for sure."

"Which way?"

He pointed west toward the mountains.

I snapped my seat belt in, my hand poised to shift gears to drive. "Let's go," I said to Bob, moving into action. "Can you pull out the map in the glove compartment?"

I focused on the road as Bob rummaged through the compartment, grunting when he found it. "Got it."

In case I needed it, I kept a folded map in my car, which had come in handy when the cell signal was weak, or I couldn't access the maps app on my phone.

"Make a right turn at Rocky Road to get to Route 82. We can also go on the back roads, but the straight shot is the fastest."

In a few minutes, we were on Route 82. "Where's Drew going, do you know?" I asked.

"Beats me," Bob said.

"You suppose he was going to meet Sallie Rae, or she was going to meet him?"

"Maybe they had something to do."

I racked my brain. I vaguely recalled Sallie Rae had mentioned she'd gone hiking with Drew a while back, but my attention span was short, and I wished I'd paid more attention to what she'd said.

"You been up to the mountains?" I asked.

"Yes. I've gone hiking, but most of it is rough terrain."

I turned to look at him, a sinking feeling gathering in the pit of my stomach. How were we going to find them in the mountains? Besides, I had an aversion to snakes, truth be told.

"Uh, you okay with snakes?" I asked.

Bob threw me a reassuring smile. "Believe it or not, they want you to leave them alone as much as you do."

"Really?" I needed assurance.

"Yup, really. Don't go trampling where you're not supposed to, and watch your feet."

My eyes on the road, I tried to dispel images of wiggly snakes slithering on the ground, intertwined on branches, or dangling from the tree limbs.

CHAPTER FIVE

I HAD DREAMED OF A MOUNTAIN RECENTLY. IT ROSE toward the heavens, mighty and majestic, the top portion shrouded by mist and clouds. It was ethereal. Weird. I'd rubbed my eyes. The swirling mist had teased me as I strained to catch a glimpse of the mountain top. My unsettled stomach churned, keeping me trapped in the dream. I couldn't find clarity or meaning, no matter how much I tossed and turned. I tried to leave, but something kept me there as my fears surrounded me, and I was afraid of confronting them.

I didn't mention my dream to Bob as we headed west in my ratty, old car. This was broad daylight. What could go wrong? I swept away the nagging thoughts and shook my head as a calming voice soothed, *It was only a dream.*

Bob leaned over and peered at my dashboard. "Fuel's getting dangerously low. We're almost out."

"Oh, no. I hope there's a gas station nearby," I said, nervously checking the gauge needle.

Bob did a search on his phone, and the closest one that popped up was at the next exit, about four miles down the highway. It seemed like an eternity, but five minutes later, I pulled into the gas station and screeched to a stop at the first gas pump.

"I'll run in and grab some snacks and bottled water. See if there are other supplies we might need," Bob said.

I jumped out and lifted the nozzle to pump the gas, catching sight of a breathtaking view as I stood there. The mountain loomed, appearing closer now that I was not behind the windshield. A chill ran down my spine. I fumbled and dropped the gas nozzle, the metal handle clanking loudly as it landed on the concrete pad, yanking the hose.

"Hey, you okay?" came a rumbling voice. It belonged to a strapping man.

I stared into a pair of inquisitive, dark brown eyes framed under thick brows in a rugged face. I dropped my gaze, staring at the man's shirt with rolled-up sleeves, worn jeans splattered with mud, and boots. I watched the movement of his muscular arm and long fingers, reaching to grab the nozzle.

"You want gas?" He removed the gas cap on my car.

I must have nodded. He dropped the nozzle in my gas tank with a loud thud, snapping me out of my daze.

"I'm ... er," I mumbled as he pulled up on the nozzle's trigger and flipped the lock. Vexed with myself for losing it in front of a total stranger, I glanced around, noticing the black truck parked behind my car. "Sorry to hold you up."

"No problem."

"Thank you." I returned a weak smile, managing to put on a good front.

"You drivin'?" he asked.

"Yes, with a friend."

"Where you headed?"

I waved vaguely in the direction of the mountain.

He frowned and glanced at my clothes. "You ain't dressed for hikin'."

"Oh no, just passing that way."

I saw the way he looked at me as if he was trying to figure me out or he didn't believe me.

"What's the name of the mountain?" I asked.

"The locals call it Snake Mountain."

I swallowed and gulped a couple of times. "You know the area?" The quiver in my voice was unmistakable.

"Like the back of my hand," he said. "Don't get lost. There's an old hut partway up the mountain if you need to rest and you don't know your way around."

I saw Bob striding out of the gas station, carrying a couple of bags, and coming our way.

"This is my friend, Bob," I said, a warm smile spreading across my face.

His eyes traveled in Bob's direction.

"I'm Eve, by the way. What's your name?"

He hesitated for a brief second. "Steve."

I decided to take a leap of faith. I pulled out my cell phone and showed him a picture of Sallie Rae and Drew. I'd snapped it from the photo on her desk. It was taken at a party and not the best shot. But it was all I had at the moment.

"Ever seen these two people?"

Steve frowned. "Who are they?"

"Our friends. We're looking for them."

He moved in for a closer look. "Can't say I have."

"Well, thanks, Steve." I flashed him a smile before opening the passenger's side door, signaling Bob to take the driver's seat.

"I hope you don't mind driving."

Bob chuckled.

"What was that all about?" he asked when we'd slid in and buckled our seat belts. I told Bob about the conversation with Steve back at the gas station. He listened intently and didn't make any comments.

Solid as a rock—the phrase popped up in my mind —dependable, calm, strong. Bob wasn't a talker, but he was a friend I could count on, especially if we were headed toward Snake Mountain.

I checked my messages while he drove. I had a missed call from Mrs. Landon. She'd left a voicemail with her address, asking us to stop by and see her. I returned her call, but she didn't answer. I left a voicemail as well.

"Change of plans," I said. "Mrs. Landon called, and she wants to see us. We could go see her first."

"How far is it?"

I gave Bob the address and put it in my cell.

We'd arrived at a crossroads where the highway veered around the mountain, and another road ran straight ahead. I checked the maps. "Keep on Route 82. We should be there in about an hour."

CHAPTER SIX

A WOMAN PEERED FROM THE WINDOW AS WE PULLED into the driveway of the modest bungalow. The pulled-back curtain swayed as it was released.

Bob parked, and we walked to the front door. It swung open before we could knock.

"Mrs. Landon?" I managed to say before she grabbed my arm.

"You must be Eve." Her hands clutched me as her pleading eyes darted across my face. I got the distinct impression she was desperate. But I didn't have any answers for her, only questions.

"Yes. And this is my friend, Bob," I said.

She glanced at him and tipped her head, then turned back to me.

"Please come in," she said, releasing my arm as she led the way.

The darkened living room was gloomy, the heavy curtains drawn closed. She gestured to the couch, faded to an undetectable hue. We sat.

"Oh, where are my manners?" she muttered. "Would you like something to drink?"

"I'm fine," I said. I held my back straight, legs uncrossed.

Bob shook his head. The man of few words said nothing. I could've used his help now.

"Any word from Sallie Rae?" I asked.

"This isn't like her, you know." Mrs. Landon ran a hand through her gray-streaked hair. A quick, jerky movement. She fidgeted in the armchair, a blank look pasted on her weary face. I couldn't tell if she was lost in thought or what she was thinking.

From what I gathered, she was overprotective of her only daughter. The two had always been close. Sallie Rae's father had left before Sallie Rae was born. Life hadn't been easy for her as a single parent. But Mrs. Landon provided for her child, making sure there was food on the table, clothes on her back, and a place to call home. If Sallie Rae felt deprived or resentful, she didn't show it. Sallie Rae exuded a happy personality, the kind that attracted people to her—the wide-eyed, fresh-faced girl with the engaging smile. And she was smart. Smart enough to get a scholarship and a ticket out of town.

"You haven't been able to reach her?" I asked.

Mrs. Landon shook her head. "I don't know where she is. I've called, but there's no answer. Her roommate hasn't seen her. This ... this is so unlike her." Her voice trailed to a whisper. "She's all I have."

I reached over to squeeze her hand. "Can you think of anything she said or did that may give us a clue?"

"The last time we talked, it was short, and she cut off abruptly. I thought she didn't sound like her usual chirpy self, but there was noise in the background. My hearing isn't what it used to be."

"You didn't start to worry until you couldn't reach her?" Bob asked.

Mrs. Landon blinked, turning to him. "Yes, you're right. My Sallie Rae's a good girl, and she's always returned my calls."

"Would you mind showing us her room?" I asked politely.

"Anything to help. The sheriff sent his deputy here and another guy. They've looked." Mrs. Landon stood up, and we followed her.

She paused before the closed door. "I still straighten up her room between visits. Sallie Rae used to say it looked like a hotel room." A brief smile momentarily brightened up her face. "I used to work as a motel maid, and that's how I made her bed. She got a kick out of that ... said it was special."

Mrs. Landon opened Sallie Rae's bedroom door, and we trailed in close behind her. Unlike her college room, this place was neat and orderly.

"I do her laundry and wash the sheets after each visit. She keeps sets of clothes here so that she doesn't have to pack them. Sallie Rae likes to travel light," Mrs. Landon said.

A dresser, twin bed, table, and chair occupied the room. A solitary doll in a pink lace dress propped up and positioned on the neatly-folded bed linens provided a clue it was a girl's room, along with a smattering of trinkets, hair clips, headbands, and a pink hairbrush on the dresser top.

It was home, but it didn't exude warmth and fuzziness. Despite the attempts to give it a lived-in, cozy feeling, I got the impression it was more like a forlorn room for an occasional visitor traveling through town.

CHAPTER SEVEN

WHEN WE LEFT MRS. LANDON'S HOUSE, I BOLTED DOWN the steps. Perhaps it was the darkened rooms or the melancholy that seemed to permeate everything. It was so depressing. I had to get away. Outside in the sunshine, I sucked in a deep breath of fresh air.

"If you don't mind driving …," I said as I grabbed the passenger door handle, glaring at it, impatient for Bob to unlock the car and get moving.

He gave me a bemused look and shook his head. Rays of sunlight played peekaboo in Bob's unruly thatch of thick brown hair. I had a strong urge to run my fingers through it. I laughed. Just like that, he lifted my mood.

"Door's open," he said.

I hopped in my car and buckled the seat belt. I leaned back and heaved deep breaths.

"Better?" he asked, this man of few words. I sensed Bob understood. He had this calming effect on me.

I rubbed my throbbing temple. Since Mrs. Landon's

call woke me up early this morning, I'd been deprived of my sleep and out of sorts. This place made it worse. I had to cut and run before my headache worsened.

"Where to?" Bob asked.

"Mrs. Landon didn't have much to add, but she mentioned Sallie Rae took a job here this summer working for Dr. Parker. Let's check it out." I mapped it on my cell and provided the directions. "It's five minutes away."

The doctor's office occupied the entire first floor in an older house. According to Mrs. Landon, he'd opened the practice in a small, one-room office. A hometown doc, Dr. Parker had been a fixture here for over thirty years. His long-time receptionist had trained her daughter Kelly as a replacement when she retired a couple of years ago. Later, when Kelly needed time off for her pregnancy and the birth of the new baby, the doc opened a temporary position in the summer. Sallie Rae got wind of it from her old friend Kelly and went for it. She interviewed and got the job.

The sign with Dr. Parker's name was prominently placed in front of the freshly-painted house. Bob spun the car into a mostly-vacant parking lot and parked. I bounced out of the car, opened the front door, and entered the office with Bob close behind me.

The receptionist behind the counter cast a glance at us as we approached.

"Hi." She beamed a smile.

My eyes traveled to the neatly-pinned name tag on her shirt—Kelly. I connected the stray hairs and a hint of tiredness in her dull eyes to her new motherhood status, wondering if she was up all night with her new baby.

"My name is Eve Sawyer, and this is Bob Harding. I'm a school friend of Sallie Rae's." I returned the smile. "Mrs. Landon mentioned you grew up together with her daughter and stayed good friends after she left for college."

Kelly nodded. "I stayed in town and married my high school sweetheart. We kept in touch. I just had a baby. Sallie Rae helped me out. Worked here in the summer while I was out on maternity leave."

"Mrs. Landon reported her daughter missing when she didn't show up at home this weekend. She hasn't been able to reach her. She called me to help, and we wanted to see if you might know something about where she is."

Kelly's jaw dropped when I said the word "missing."

"Look, we're trying to figure out where she could be. What might have happened," I said.

"This is so unlike Sallie Rae. She comes home a lot, you know, being so close to her mom."

"Has Sallie Rae confided in you?" I asked.

Kelly glanced away. She frowned.

"This summer was tough for her. Being away from her boyfriend."

"Drew?"

She nodded. "Sallie Rae felt boxed in. Her mom ... she means well, but she put a lot of pressure on Sallie Rae." Kelly stared at me, lips pressed. Finally, shaking her head, she said, "Guilt-tripped her into staying here."

As I waited for Kelly to continue, I reflected. I was

about the same age as Sallie Rae, but I didn't go home often. I was lucky my mom didn't pry and quiz me. She knew better. That sort of thing would drive me nuts and push me away. Over the years, we'd worked out terms we could both live with.

"I was selfish, too." Kelly sighed. "I wanted Sallie Rae to help while I was on leave."

"You think she disappeared to get away from it all?" I asked.

"She hasn't sounded like her usual chipper self lately."

I glanced at Bob. He remained silent.

"Look, if you think of anything, any little thing, here's my number," I said as I passed it to Kelly.

CHAPTER EIGHT

WE LEFT AND DROVE AROUND TOWN, PASSING A SMALL print shop.

"We should make a missing person flyer," I said.

"There's a café up ahead." Bob pointed to a sign by the side of the road. "You got your laptop?"

Coffee and food sounded good. I could do with that.

"Perfect. I have my laptop in the backseat," I said, turning around to reach for my backpack and then grinning. "You can help me design the flyer."

Bob grunted.

We were seated right away when the waitress spotted us in the front entry area. We ordered coffee and sandwiches for lunch, egg salad for me and tuna for Bob. I loved to eat in country diners serving tasty, home-cooked meals.

I finished first. Pushing the dishes out of the way, I whipped out my laptop and turned it on.

"We can make copies at the print shop down the

street and give some flyers to Mrs. Landon before we leave."

"You have a picture?" Bob asked.

I pulled out my cell and showed Bob the photo I snapped of the picture on her desk of Sallie Rae and Drew together. They were at a party, the two of them laughing and having fun. Sallie Rae was glowing and crazy in love. Drew's head was tilted, snug against hers. It wasn't the best picture, but it captured the mood of their relationship. And it was a beautiful photo of Sallie Rae.

"Should we crop out Drew?"

Bob studied the photo close up. "Why not do two flyers?"

"Cropped and uncropped?"

"Yes ... in case he's missing too," Bob said.

CHAPTER NINE

IT TOOK US MOST OF THE DAY TO GET EVERYTHING DONE. On the way out of town, we stopped at the sheriff's office and talked to the deputy on duty, Chat Walkins. We left a few copies of the flyer, and I let him know Mrs. Landon had asked us to help. The deputy said they'd been working with Mrs. Landon and had also contacted Midway College campus security. Mrs. Landon also promised she'd let us know if she heard anything when we dropped off a few flyers at her house.

Bob offered to drive back to college, stopping to put up flyers in gas stations and convenience stores along Route 82. I was grateful. I'd been caught up with the activities of the day and was stressed out, hanging on with adrenaline. Now the tiredness took over. I slumped in my seat, exhausted and drained, the heaviness in my eyelids pulling them down, lower and lower. I was babbling to Bob as I struggled to keep awake long enough to say, "Please wake me if anything happens." Then I closed my eyes and slipped into dreamland.

§

SOMEONE IS SHOUTING MY NAME.

I pivot my body around until I've made a complete circle. The voice is vaguely familiar, though I don't see anyone yet.

I open my mouth to call out, but I can't speak. I stir up noise with my feet as leaves crunch underneath. I stamp my feet, jump, and wave my arms.

Where is this place? I'm in a forest, so dense the sunlight has to fight for space. My heart is pounding, and my first reaction is to run. But the voice draws me back, calling to me.

My feet don't know which direction to move. Then there's a hissing. My eyes widen as a snake crawls over my shoes. I want to fling it off, toss it with my shoe far to the side. I stand petrified. Then more snakes come, slithering and gathering en masse. The hissing grows louder and louder as the snakes make their way up my legs, arms, belly, chest, and neck. I let out a blood-curdling scream.

§

"EVE!" I woke up to Bob's face inches away, brows knitted, shaking me with intensity and urgency. I'd never seen him act this way before.

"Eve," he repeated.

"What ... what happened?" I rubbed my eyes.

"You were having a nightmare," he said, "and screaming."

I stared at him. It was coming back to me now. We were in my car, on our way home. He was driving. But wait, we were stopped now. One look out the window confirmed the car had been pulled over on the side of the road.

"Bad dream?"

I nodded. Even in broad daylight, I shuddered.

"You're okay now," Bob said.

His deep, calm voice had a soothing and relaxing effect on me. I was relieved that he didn't ask me to relive my terrifying dream and talk about it.

"Say it again," I said.

A grin replaced the worried frown. "You're okay now," he said, adding, "You're safe here. It was only a bad dream. You're safe now, Eve."

I smiled at my friend, grateful for his kindness.

CHAPTER TEN

Bob called the next morning while I was at home, sipping a mug of coffee—a strong, dark Italian roast, no cream or sugar. My hair was still damp from the shower. I was so exhausted last night that I passed out the minute my head hit the pillow.

"Good morning," I chirped.

"I've got a lead." Bob got straight to the point. No small talk first, asking me how I slept.

I sat up straight, clutching the phone to my ear. "A lead?"

A sudden knock made me jump.

"Open the door."

"What ... are you outside now?" I shrieked.

I jumped up and looked out the living room window. Sure enough, his truck was parked in front. Geez. If I hadn't had my coffee yet, it'd be too early. I twisted the doorknob and swung open the front door.

"This better be good," I said.

Bob stood on the doorstep, hesitating, shifting his feet.

I smiled. "Well, don't just stand there. C'mon in."

In a minute, I had him sitting at the table with a fresh cup of coffee.

"One of the guys, Matt, who works part-time at the grocery store, called."

"And?" I interrupted. Now, I was the impatient one.

"He claimed he saw Sallie Rae."

"When?"

"Friday afternoon."

"Is he working there now?" I asked.

Bob nodded. "Every weekend."

"Let's go talk to him."

MATT WAS STOCKING the shelves in the canned-soup area when we arrived. It wasn't hard to find him in the mom-and-pop grocery store. After a round of introductions, I told him why we were there and asked if he's willing to talk to us about Sallie Rae.

"Sure, what you wanna know?" Matt said.

"About what time did you see Sallie Rae on Friday?" I asked.

"Oh, around three in the afternoon."

"Did you check your watch?"

"Didn't have to. I clock in at three."

"Where did you see her?"

"Aisle ten. Candy and snacks."

"Did you speak?"

"I was passing by, and she turned to ask me a question."

"Which was—"

"About chocolates ... She had one in each hand, and she was trying to decide which one to buy."

"Did she seem upset, sad?"

"Well, she didn't say, but her eyes looked a bit puffy, and she was digging in her purse for tissues."

"What did you say about the chocolates?"

"Said I like the dark chocolate with almonds."

"The other one was what?"

"Milk chocolate with caramel."

"Which one did she get?"

"The dark."

"Anything else?"

"She thanked me and rushed off like she was in a hurry."

"Thank you," I said, catching Bob's eye as we left.

I added Matt's name to the list of persons we had spoken to. Flipping to a blank page in my notepad, I wrote "TIMELINE" across the top, and underneath it, "Friday 3 p.m.," and Matt's name, underlined.

We still didn't know why Sallie Rae went missing, where she was, or if she was alive or dead.

CHAPTER ELEVEN

SALLIE RAE WAS A SMALL-TOWN GIRL. A POPULAR, WELL-liked college student. She was your average B to B-plus student. She didn't have lofty aspirations to become the president or be famous or wealthy. Her hopes and wants were simple: to finish college, get married, buy a house with a white picket fence, and have babies—in that order. As for having a career, she'd wanted to delay it for a few years until her yet-to-be born babies were old enough to go to school. Family came first. This was her way of thinking. Like the mama bear, a fierce protector of her family. Of course, love would be the glue keeping everything together. And when she fell in love, she'd fall in all the way. Deep.

I couldn't help thinking about the picture on her desk and cheering for Sallie Rae, her happiness, her future. Barely into adulthood, she had her whole life to look forward to after graduation. But that was before *this* happened, before she went missing. I knew this much about missing people: The initial period of time was crucial. The more time that passed, the likelihood of finding the person diminished, along with the prospect of finding the person alive.

My stomach twisted at the thought of Sallie Rae in pain, bleeding, and injured ... or something worse. Had someone silenced her? My body shook involuntarily as I wondered what could have happened. I couldn't let her down.

Sallie Rae needed all the help she could get.

Bob and I came up with a plan. We sprang into action, contacting everyone on our list, emailing our flyers to them, and asking them to please share them around campus. I submitted a short piece for the college newspaper's online edition—and it would likely be tweeted and shared on their social media posts.

I reached out to Professor Reynolds in the journalism department. I knew he had long-standing contacts in the local media. He agreed to help get the word out and said anyone with information would be asked to contact the authorities.

We didn't know if Sallie Rae ever left town, and if so, how far she went before she disappeared or if she remained close to home. There were too many questions we didn't have answers to. Time was of the essence, and we were racing to find answers. The clock was ticking.

My cell phone rang, and I recognized the number.

"Any news yet?" Mrs. Landon asked.

"No," I said. I didn't believe in giving people false hope. I brought her up to date on our activities. I had a question for her, though.

"The fall break is this week, starting on Wednesday." I paused a moment, then asked, "I'm wondering why Sallie Rae would have been going home this weekend. It doesn't make sense. Why didn't she wait a few days to go home on a long fall break weekend instead?"

Mrs. Landon sighed. "Sallie Rae had her mind made up. It was this weekend or no weekend. She was firm about it. I asked her what was so important, but she didn't say."

"You think she had other plans?"

Mrs. Landon screeched, then hacked and coughed.

The sound grated on my nerves. Maybe she ought to get it checked out. It'd be depressing to stay in that dreary, dark house and be hacking and coughing away. Maybe Sallie Rae wanted to have some fun for a change. Maybe she had a change of mind and disappeared. Maybe she had something better to do.

CHAPTER TWELVE

FALL BREAK THIS WEEK MEANT ONLY TWO DAYS OF classes, on Monday and Tuesday. I had finished my projects and turned them in online. The only thing left was a midterm exam on Monday morning. I wasn't worried, though, since my grade-point average was in great shape. I was tempted to skip my last class on Tuesday, and I wouldn't be the only one.

I loved watching the leaves turn colors to rich shades of spectacular yellow, orange, and red, and in between. I loved plump pumpkins with carved, toothless smiles; yummy pumpkin spiced lattes, pies, cakes, and breads; fall harvests, scarecrows, and festivals; and hot apple cider, roasted corn, wood fires, and the fresh, cool air of crisp autumn days. It was a glorious time of the year, with the rising anticipation of the holidays around the corner.

The ring of an incoming call startled me. My mind had been elsewhere—daydreaming.

"Hello?" I said, staring at the strange number, focusing on it.

"Oh hi, this is Kelly. We met yesterday at Dr. Parker's office ... and you said to call you if I remembered anything."

I switched instantly to alert mode. "Yes, at the doctor's office." A vision of Kelly, the new mother, sleep-deprived and stressed, popped up. I remembered our short conversation.

"After you left, I got to thinking," Kelly said.

I waited, raising an eyebrow she couldn't see.

"Sallie Rae had asked me about something a while back. You know, since I work in a doctor's office."

"Was she ill?"

"Oh no, nothing like that."

"So, what?"

"She was asking about DNA tests."

"What did you say?"

"I could tell she'd done a fair amount of research already from the questions she asked." Kelly paused. "We don't test here, but I helped her find some credible genetic-testing sites."

"Did she follow through?"

"Yes."

"Did Sallie Rae ever mention why she did it?"

"She'd been curious about the father she never knew. She wanted to find him. Her dream was for her father to walk her down the aisle one day, and they'd all be together as one happy family."

"Did her mother talk about her father?"

"Not that I know of. Sallie Rae had been asking for

years and finally got tired of banging her head against a wall. She took it upon herself to look for him."

"By getting a DNA test—"

"Yes. And she chose the companies with the largest genealogical pools to increase the chances of finding her birth father in their databases. And they're adding new people all the time."

"They'll compare their DNAs to hers?"

"Yes. When she gets her results back, she can get in touch with her matches. You've heard of people finding missing relatives. Well, she's determined to track down her father."

"Then what happened?" I asked.

"I had my baby, and we didn't discuss it again."

"Thanks for calling. I appreciate it." I hung up, making a mental note of it.

CHAPTER THIRTEEN

I MADE A FRESH POT OF COFFEE, POURED A CUP, AND settled down to study for my midterm tomorrow, spreading my textbooks and notes out on the kitchen table. I turned off my cell phone to give myself a couple of hours of uninterrupted peace and quiet and dived into the study of human body structure and functions, amazed at the complexity of it all and how the systems worked together. For the time being, I pushed all thoughts of Sallie Rae away to concentrate on my studying.

I'd been so absorbed in reading that I didn't realize my cup was empty until I reached for it. Dried rings of brown stained the bottom. I got up and walked to the kitchen to refill my coffee, stretch my legs, and take a quick break.

Five minutes later, I hit the books again. I'd taken meticulous notes in class and highlighted words and passages. Physiology was one subject I'd never cram. I was interested in it, and I'd kept up with class; nevertheless, I still needed to study. After another hour or so, I plopped my pencil down. The plunk as it landed on the stack of papers produced a satisfying sound, easing my anxiety and stress level and releasing a bit of the heaviness from my shoulders.

It also cleared my mind to focus on Sallie Rae.

I called Bob.

"Any new leads?" I asked.

"Nope," he said.

"You want to take a break from studying?" I asked.

Bob was more organized than I could ever be. It was in the nature of his DNA. I'd bet he was so well prepared, he could take his exams now. He wasn't the type to wing it, and I doubted he stressed over exams like I did.

"What's on your mind?" he asked.

"I've been trying to reach Drew since we went over to his place yesterday. Have you or any of the guys heard from him?"

"Nope."

"It's odd. I'm worried about him too. You free to go over there?" I asked.

"Meet you in ten minutes," Bob replied.

RANDALL QUINN, Drew's roommate, was at home when we arrived. Bob had texted him, so he was expecting us.

I knocked on the door.

Randall opened it and cracked a pasted-on smile

when he saw us. He wore a wrinkled shirt, and his hair was disheveled.

"Hi, Randall," I said, a faint smile lifting my lips.

"Come in." He led us to the kitchen table, pulled out two distressed wooden chairs, and waved for Bob and me to sit.

"Thank you." I watched as he disappeared into the back bedroom and came back with another one for himself and sat.

"You know why we're here?" I asked.

He squirmed in his chair like he was restless or uneasy.

"Sallie Rae is missing, and we can't reach Drew. Have you heard from him?"

"Not since he texted me."

"When?"

"Yesterday, he said something came up, and he had to cancel."

"Cancel?"

"Yeah, somebody posted a couch and coffee table for sale. It was cheap. We were going to see them yesterday."

"Did he say what came up?"

"Nope. I called him later, but he didn't answer or call me back." Randall clenched his jaw. In a quick, jerky motion, he scooped up his stack of books and tossed them on the floor, grunting with exertion. He dragged his mismatched chair closer, scraping the legs on the worn floor. As he leaned over to clear some more space on the cluttered table, he pushed aside the pile of mail I saw yesterday, sending a flurry of letters flying and toppling to the floor.

I reached down to grab them up and glimpsed a utility bill and some junk mail on top. Underneath, an envelope caught my attention, with handwritten words carefully printed on the back, across the sealed flap. I flipped it over. There was no stamp; it was probably dropped in the mailbox. It was addressed to Drew Walker. I gasped.

CHAPTER FOURTEEN

I BLINKED RAPIDLY, STARING AT THE NAME NEATLY printed in the return address area.

"Who's it from?" Randall leaned forward across the table, his butt raised from the chair.

"Sallie Rae," I sucked in a quick breath and took a closer look.

"Look at this!" I shouted, shoving it toward him. "Have you seen it?"

Randall frowned. "I don't look through the mail. I toss them on the pile. Drew ... he takes care of the utility bills. We split them. He tells me how much, and I pay him my portion."

"When was the last time you saw Drew?" I asked.

"Friday," Randall said, rubbing his jaw.

"What time?" Bob asked.

"In the morning before I left for class."

"What about later? Was he here?" I persisted.

"Dunno, I didn't come home until late."

"Did Drew say anything about Sallie Rae? Has he done anything odd?"

Randall leaned back in his chair. "Well ... he's acted nervous."

"What do you mean?"

"I came into his room, startled him. Drew was staring intently at the screen on his laptop, and he didn't hear me."

"Did you see the screen?"

"I caught sight of a mug shot, a guy."

"What'd he look like?"

"Mean," Randall spat. "Cropped hair, rugged face, scraggly and unshaven."

"Age?" Bob asked.

"I'd say in his forties."

"Who was it?" I said.

"I asked, but Drew clammed up and closed his laptop." Randall paused, adding, "It wasn't any of my business, you know."

My cell phone vibrated. I had flipped it to mute during my study session and left it on silent.

"Gotta take this call. It's Mrs. Landon." I moved away to the front room to talk to her.

"Eve," she said when I answered, "I have news." She spoke quickly.

My heartbeat quickened. Was it good news?

"They found Sallie Rae's car."

"And Sallie Rae?" My words hung in the air, heavy between us. What had the sheriff's office told Mrs. Landon?

She hesitated before she answered. "Not yet, but she

called me." I felt something was off. Mrs. Landon didn't sound elated and excited, but subdued and worried. Something else was going on she hadn't told me.

I took a breath to let this sink in. "You ... you talked to Sallie Rae? When?"

"She called me this morning."

"What'd she say?" I asked calmly.

"It was a brief call. She knew we were looking for her. Called to tell me she's fine."

"That's it?"

"Pretty much. She said she needs some time away."

"How long?"

"She ... she didn't say."

"She's not coming home now?"

This time, Mrs. Landon's sob came through loud and clear.

"She sounded okay, right?" I tried to soothe her. At least, we knew she was alive.

"I don't know ..." Her answer came across muffled.

"Where was the car?" I asked.

"In the back of a gas station."

I did a quick mental recap of our driving route. We had stopped at several gas stations to post the flyers after we left Mrs. Landon's home on the way back to campus on Route 82.

"Which gas station?"

"Three exits from my house."

I had a light-bulb moment. "Sallie Rae called from the gas station?"

"Yes. The number showed up on the call, and the authorities traced it."

"Why wouldn't she use her cell phone?"

"She said she'd turned it off. So that would explain why Sallie Rae didn't get my calls and the messages I'd left."

I didn't point out the obvious to Mrs. Landon that Sallie Rae could've turned a cell phone back on, out of consideration for her feelings. "Hmm, maybe she didn't want anyone to ping her cell and track her location?"

"Could be. That makes sense."

"What's the next step?"

"They will go over Sallie Rae's car to check it out thoroughly."

"Will they continue to search for Sallie Rae?"

"I ... no, the missing person search has been called off—after I talked to Sallie Rae at the gas station and she said she's fine. She's just not ready to come home yet."

Before I hung up, I promised Mrs. Landon I'd find out what I could.

I walked back to the kitchen. Randall was having an animated conversation with Bob and doing most of the talking. No surprise there. They stopped when they saw me. Saw my face.

"They found Sallie Rae's car at a gas station," I said.

"Oh my God, is Sallie Rae okay?" Randall asked.

"She called her mom and said she's fine. They're checking her car."

"They who?"

"The sheriff's office." I tucked my thumb in my jeans pocket. "I'm going there."

"When?" Bob asked.

"In the morning, after my nine o'clock exam."

"I'm coming with you. Meet you around ten," Bob said.

Randall fidgeted in his chair. "I have two tests in the morning. You guys wait for me, okay? Around noon?"

"You'd be a big help here if Drew calls or comes back home," I said soothingly. I could tell Randall was itching to go too.

"He doesn't have his phone."

I stared at him. "Where is it?"

Randall got up, walked to the bedroom, and came back with a cell phone in his hand. He plunked it on the table.

I picked up the phone. The screen was black even as I held down the power button and tried to reboot it. "Phone's dead. Probably ran out of charge." I handed it back to Randall. "Do you think we can try to get into it, see if there are any messages on the lock screen?"

"No, I think it'll require his passcode after restarting, and I don't have it."

CHAPTER FIFTEEN

I WOKE UP THE NEXT MORNING FEELING DISJOINTED. I hadn't slept well during the night. The sense of hope and dread tore at me and pulled me in different directions. I dressed in comfortable clothes, an old button-down cotton shirt and pale blue wash-worn jeans, and tossed extra pencils in my backpack. I slung it over my shoulder, snatched a jacket, and carried my coffee out to the car.

Outside, storm clouds hung overhead, interspersed by patches of gray sky and slivers of sunlight shining through gaps. It was a short drive to campus, and I arrived early for my exam. I made use of the extra time and did some last-minute cramming before nine.

I was done at ten and walked out to my car. A few minutes later, Bob drove up after his own test.

"Hop in," he said, rolling down the window of his truck.

Grabbing my backpack and stuffing my jacket

inside, I locked my car and jumped into his rickety-looking but well-maintained truck.

I closed my eyes and laid my head back on the seat as Bob drove. Except for the quiet hum of the motor, I was left alone with my thoughts, my attention focused on Sallie Rae. Her mother hadn't called me today. I checked my cell phone. No missed calls. No texts. No voicemails.

I rummaged in my backpack and found my pencil, popped it in my mouth, and promptly chomped on it. The familiar habit of sinking my teeth into the wood was comforting. I chewed like a crazy woman at first. Fast and furious. Then I slowed down. It'd be no good if I ran out of smooth, unmarked territory. But I'd bought extras at the bookstore. All set for a good while.

Sometimes thoughts popped up while I chewed. When in a bind, couldn't see a way out, or was going around in circles—two plus two equals four, but so does one plus three, and three plus one, and zero plus four, and four plus zero.

Questions swirled in my head. On the one hand, I was relieved Sallie Rae was alive. On the other hand, I couldn't help wondering, where was she? How long would she be gone? What was she doing? Why? Where was Drew?

I looked out the car window. The clouds hung heavy and obscured the blue sky. It was the kind of dreary day that could turn into rain or just be cloudy. I didn't bring my umbrella, so I prayed it would stay dry. I prayed for Sallie Rae.

It was comforting to have Bob drive. I wasn't all

there yet. Troubling thoughts swirled in my mind, not letting me go. I turned to Bob, noticing his eyes were straight ahead and focused on the road.

"What are you thinking?" I asked.

"What's going on in that head of yours?" Bob threw back at me.

I chuckled. "You don't want to know."

"Do share."

"What do you make of it? ... Sallie Rae's call and where her car is?"

"First of all, she's alive."

"Yes."

"We know the last place she was alive—at the gas station."

"True."

"And she had driven there."

I could see how Bob was going at this, in his analytical and methodical way.

"So, big clues," I said. "Mrs. Landon said the sheriff's office has her car and is checking it out. What else?"

"She's fine. And she isn't ready to come home yet."

I nodded. "But she didn't say why she needs time away or for how long."

"I bet she's still in the area."

I reacted, pushing outward from the seat belt until it restrained me. "She *couldn't* have gone far ... not without her car."

"Not unless she had other means of transportation."

"Great point, Bob. Do you think she's with Drew?"

He shrugged.

"What kind of car does Drew drive?" I asked.

"A VW."

"Color?"

"White."

"Sallie Rae may be alone or with someone else—like Drew." I pulled up the map on my cell phone to Route 82. "Mrs. Landon said the gas station was three exits from her house. Let's start there."

"Sounds like a good plan." Bob threw me a goofy smile. If his intent was to cheer me up and pull me out of the doldrums and push me into action, then he got an A.

CHAPTER SIXTEEN

AFTER DIGGING INTO MY BACKPACK AND PULLING OUT MY notebook, I zoomed in on my phone's map, counted the exits from Midway College to Mrs. Landon's house on Route 82, and made a note of it.

"It's a straight shot on Route 82," I said.

Bob glanced at the map. "The day we posted the flyers along the highway was a whirlwind. I'm sure we stopped at every exit, but right now, I can't remember which one it was or what the gas stations looked like until we see them."

"I'll give you the directions."

"How far are we?"

I checked my phone. "About thirty-four minutes out."

My heart was pounding so hard I thought I'd have a heart attack. I gripped my phone, silently cursing the slow crawl of the clock. My imagination was running wild, fearing the worst. I thought about the situation. "We don't know why she's not going home," I said.

"Or who she's with, if anyone," Bob said.

"Do you think she's in danger?"

Bob shrugged. I was getting used to the strong, silent type. I knew he talked—I just had to tease it out of him. He didn't jabber like some guys I'd tune out.

We drove in silence. I used the time to do some searches on my phone until the voice on the map app announced the turn, counting down the distance to the exit.

My heart fluttered. I looked out the car windows on both sides and in front, half expecting to see Sallie Rae.

Bob slowed down before the exit. The sign for the solitary gas station pointed left, and he turned that way. Route 82 didn't have several gas stations clustered around exits, unlike the major highways. Some of the exits didn't even have gas stations. The one here was an older building. It had two pumps.

He drove up to a spot in front and parked. I didn't see any signs of police presence.

We got out and walked around. I checked the back of the building and didn't see Sallie Rae's car. "Let's go in," I said.

The bell dinged as I pushed open the door. The interior was spartan, one side lined with rows of shelves. The clerk standing behind the counter watched as we entered. A sheet of plastic separated him from the customers.

I walked right up to him, noticing the frayed, white shirt and rolled-up sleeves. From the way he sat, I couldn't tell how tall he was. He appeared to be in his late teens or early twenties, thin face with a light stubble. Probably not his first job.

"Hi," I said. I didn't remember seeing him the day when we passed out the flyers. I scanned the walls for the flyer.

He eyed us as we approached.

"Help you?" he asked.

I spotted it on the counter, taped on the side, and clearly visible when someone went to pay. I pointed to the flyer.

He frowned.

I smiled. "Hi, I'm Eve, and this is Bob. We left the flyer here the other day. We spoke to the other guy ... "

"Oh, ya mean Darnell, the older guy?"

"I think so."

"He ain't here today."

I smiled again like I was glad to talk to him. "We can talk to you. What's your name?"

"Billy."

"The police found Sallie Rae's car yesterday." I tapped her picture softly, the one where she was at the party with Drew, smiling. "She made a call from here. Did you see her?"

"The sheriff already asked."

"Okay. We're her friends. Can you tell us, please?"

"Yeah, she asked for change."

"For gas?"

"No, the pay phone outside."

"Did you recognize her?"

He stared at me strangely. "Nope. It's turned upside down."

It made sense. From where he sat, her photo was upside down. "So, how did you know it was her?"

"I didn't then. They came looking for her. Showed me one turned up."

"Was she alone?" Bob asked.

"Yep, came in by herself."

"Did you see her car?" I said.

"Didn't see no car."

"You worked alone?"

"Yep."

"How did she look to you?"

Billy tilted his head. "What do you mean?"

"Did she look okay?"

"She had sunglasses on."

"Do you remember what she was wearing?"

"She had on jeans and a flowery yellow top."

"She didn't look hurt or anything?"

He shook his head slowly from left to right.

I wondered if he had a visual confirmation.

"Do you have camera footage?"

He hesitated and wrinkled his forehead. "It ain't been workin' right."

Bummer. "Anything else you remember?" I was trying to jog his memory, squeezing for every bit of information.

Billy thought for a moment. "Well, she'd come up to get her quarters, ya know. She saw the flyer." He smiled like he was pleased with his recollection.

"Then, what did she do?"

"She just looked."

"Did she say anything?"

"No, but she took her time lookin'."

"You done good, Billy." I flashed a wide grin. "Thank you for your help."

CHAPTER SEVENTEEN

WE ORDERED TWO CUPS OF COFFEE-TO-GO AT THE GAS
station and got back in the car.

"What's next?" Bob asked.

I pulled up the map on my phone. "Here's where we
are, at the blue dot. Here's the next gas station about
twenty-five miles this way. In between is the
mountain."

"Snake Mountain."

"Right," I said. "If we're headed in that direction, we
could stop there."

"Just curious, why?"

"Sallie Rae had mentioned she'd gone hiking with
Drew. She wanted to get away. Maybe she was looking
for someplace quiet. Worth a look?"

Bob threw me a look. "You a hiker?"

"More of a walker. I'm not what you call an
outdoorsy type. But you are," I quickly added.

"I'm going to grab some supplies in the gas station,"
Bob said.

After Bob got what he thought we needed, we got back on Route 82. He drove for a few miles to the mountain, parked, and we got out of the truck. The rest of the way was going to be on foot. Bob divvied up the supplies between two plastic bags and handed me one. I grabbed my backpack and stuffed the supplies inside.

"We're going to come back before dark, right?" I asked, trying to keep the quiver out of my voice. I wanted Bob's reassurance. Normally I wasn't like this, but I was worried.

"Yes, there won't be time to go all the way up and down. We'll scout around a bit."

Despite his words of assurance, I kept close to Bob, my eyes trained on his lanky legs and his retreating back as he charged ahead. My shorter legs worked to keep up.

Before long, we were swallowed up in the forest, the sunlight only glimpses between the lofty treetops. The heavy foliage blocked out the rays. I felt trapped in an insular world, oblivious to the beauty around me and the sounds of the forest life. My singular goal was to catch up with Bob; I focused on him like the red point of a laser. The climb up wasn't easy. I was panting with the exertion, and sweat dripped off my forehead.

At some point, Bob stopped briefly for me to catch up. I didn't ask him to, but I sure needed it.

"Seen any signs of them yet?" I stopped short of saying snakes. I tried to shake off my fears, but they wouldn't go away. My imagination ran wild from itty bitty snakes to the green anaconda, the largest snake in the world, found in the tropical waters of South America. I'd looked this up on the National Geographic website while Bob was driving. *The scientific name is Eunectes murinus.* I'd thought they might be herbivores, but they're not. These snakes are carnivorous reptiles. I shuddered.

I knew it was a stupid question before it popped out of my mouth.

"Say again?" he asked.

I was embarrassed to realize I'd been so wrapped up in snakes that I had gotten sidetracked from our goal of looking for Sallie Rae. I quickly changed the topic, hoping Bob hadn't noticed my fears.

"Are we stopping to rest?" I asked, smiling.

"No, just a quick break for a couple of minutes."

"Remember the guy we met at the gas station?"

"You mean Steve?" He eyed me quizzically.

"Yup. When I talked to him, he mentioned there's an old hut partway up the mountain if we need to rest."

"I know the place."

"You do?"

"Us hikers know it well. I've rested there."

I flashed a grateful smile, giving a silent thanks to Steve. "How much farther?"

"Not much."

My smile widened to a grin. This bit of good news was enough to charge my batteries. I was pumped. I felt a bit of an adrenaline rush.

"Let's keep going. I want to make as much headway as possible before dark."

Now I knew why he was in such a hurry. Being

trapped on the mountain after dark was something I feared, and he knew it. I wasn't used to hiking, and I was determined not to be a holdup. I focused on the task and Bob ahead of me and marched on.

The trail we traveled on became less defined and narrower. I made up games, shoved one foot in front of the other, and counted steps. The path was littered with leaves, broken twigs, and occasional cones. The dark soil on the ground underneath was moist and yielding.

I surrendered to the serenity of the forest and fell in step, marching to the sounds of nature: insects, birds cawing, and leaves rustling. At some point, my blood pressure dropped back to normal, and my pulse slowed and steadied. I paced myself, adjusting and quickening my steps to match Bob's.

I lost all track of time. I was immersed in the tranquil beauty of the forest—the strikingly colorful wildflowers, the girth and strength of gnarly tree trunks, and the ropy roots that broke the surface of the ground. The forest and the creatures in it welcomed me into their world. I relished this peaceful, holy place I had never been to before. I feared I'd be spooked by snakes. Yet, I had not been bothered by a single one here. I'd faced my fear today.

CHAPTER EIGHTEEN

THE ATMOSPHERE CHANGED WHEN WE WALKED INTO THE clearing. Overhead, the sun's rays beamed down through the opening in the treetops. I saw the clear blue sky, unobscured, and not a trace of clouds.

Bob slowed down and stopped in front of a small structure. It looked like a hut.

"This is it," I said excitedly.

"Rest up. Take a few minutes," he said.

I slung my backpack off my shoulders and zipped it open. "What goodies did you get?"

"Water bottles and some energy bars. Got the same stuff for both of us."

"Thanks." I dug into my bag and rummaged around before deciding on a chewy bar and a bottle of water.

We sat on a wooden bench outside the small building. I wiggled my toes and stretched my legs. They weren't sore yet, but they would be by tomorrow.

"Who built this place?"

"No idea. It's a little rest stop. A place to get out of the weather when it turns bad."

I finished first and got up to take a look around the structure. Off on the side, I noticed a woodpile haphazardly arranged. I picked a few pieces up, intending to straighten up the pile. Unwittingly, I disturbed a snake, sunning on a rock next to it. I wanted to run, but I froze, my shaky legs rooted to the ground. I screamed.

Bob rushed to my side. I clutched his arm as if my life depended on it.

I pointed to the rock, jerking my arm. "Ss … sss … snake."

"Stay back." He moved closer to investigate.

He laughed as the snake slithered away, escaping. "It's gone."

"But he looked so scary," I whined, milking it for all it was worth, extracting sympathy for myself to justify making such a big deal. "What if he attacked me?"

"It's not going to hurt you. You've scared him."

"I wasn't trying to hurt or kill it."

"I know. Some people don't know it's illegal to kill non-venomous snakes here."

"Well, thanks." I continued my walk around the outside of the tiny wooden hut, making a full circle. It was built with wood logs hewn together like the ones you'd see on log cabins. There were no windows. A cut-out door created an open entrance—the only one. I walked inside.

A bench was in the middle of the floor, visible from the open doorway. I sat on the bench and faced the outside, relieved to be away from the snake, swinging my legs and wiggling my foot. The toe of my shoe kicked on a rough spot under the bench. I dismissed it and got up to leave, thinking it was probably a small rock or some kind of debris, but something pulled me back. I got on my knee and bent over to take a closer look. There was something sticking out of the dirt. Something round glittered. I reached in with my fingers and grasped it, tugging it out. I thought it might be a lost coin, but I was wrong. It wasn't.

I stared at the item pinched between my fingertips.

"Bob!" I yelled.

He dashed in.

I held it up.

"You found a ring."

I rotated the ring around. "Look again," I insisted.

"Okay ... what am I supposed to be looking at?"

"I need to wipe the dirt off. Do you have something I can use?"

"Yeah, in my backpack." He left and quickly came back with a piece of cloth.

I took it from him and rubbed off the grime, then polished the ring.

"Does it look familiar to you?" I shoved the ring closer to his face.

He scrunched his face and studied it.

I dug into my back pocket and pulled out a flyer. I held it in my right hand, and alongside it, I held the ring in my left hand.

"See?"

I held my breath. I watched him. As it slowly dawned on Bob, his face changed.

"It ... it's her ring," he whispered.

I nodded. "In the photo, you could see the ring around Sallie Rae's finger as she held up her drink."

"How do you know it's hers?"

"It's not just any ring. It's one of a kind."

"So it was special?" he asked.

My head bobbed. "Yes, it was a custom-made ring that Drew designed and commissioned. I don't think there's another ring like it." I held it tightly—a coiled serpent ring with diamonds.

"She told you?"

"In so many words. It was a big deal at school," I said. "The word had gotten out amongst us girls. We thought it might be an engagement ring, but Sallie Rae had insisted it wasn't."

I'd seen this ring on Sallie Rae's finger and recognized it immediately. What was it doing here? Tingles shot up and down my spine. I rubbed away tiny bits of dirt I'd missed, caught between the prongs and the stones, polishing it until it glowed. I sensed Sallie Rae was here, but I didn't know the reason why or what had happened. Had she confronted danger after the call to her mother to stop the search? Or did she lose possession of the ring before she made the call?

CHAPTER NINETEEN

I CALLED DEPUTY CHAT WALKINS FROM THE HUT. HE remembered me right off the bat. I told him Mrs. Landon had updated me with the latest about Sallie Rae's phone call and asked if the search team had been called off. He pretty much confirmed what I had thought. *Sallie Rae is alive, and she isn't missing.* They'd taken her off the missing persons list. Deputy Walkins had also been in touch with Midway campus police, and the authorities there were doing the same. Before I wrapped up the call with Deputy Walkins, I mentioned we'd found Sallie Rae's ring on Snake Mountain.

Sallie Rae had said she needed some time and wasn't ready to come home. I'd told the sheriff's deputy that classes would end tomorrow, followed by the beginning of the five-day fall break. On Sunday, the students would be coming back to campus. I decided to keep looking for Sallie Rae during that time. Best case scenario, she'd be back with Mrs. Landon soon. Worst case, she wouldn't show up on campus by Monday.

The mention of school reminded me to call Professor Reynolds. The announcements were on the radio about Sallie Rae. They were succinct and attention-grabbing, thanks to my mentor and teacher, whom I'd admired and had learned from immensely. He didn't answer when I called, but I left a message with an update about Sallie Rae and my conversation with the deputy.

Bob had been watching me and listening, leaning forward with one leg up, the tip of his right cowboy boot resting on the edge of the wooden bench outside the hut.

"All done?"

"One more." I held up a finger and flashed my special smile, having saved the best for last.

I called my mom and explained Sallie Rae's situation and apologized that I hadn't called earlier to firm up my own plans for fall break. I preferred to wait until I had more concrete information rather than make plans and then have to break them. A brief silence gave away her disappointment, but Mom said she would be happy to see me when I did make it. She was my chief supporter and incredibly understanding. She wasn't into guilt-tripping or being critical.

When Bob realized who I was talking to, he stepped off the bench and walked away to the edge of the clearing to give me some privacy.

I appreciated this man's patience. He had suggested stopping here, and I sure made maximum use of it. I tapped to end the call, and a thought popped up as Bob ambled toward me again. "What about you, Bob ... any plans?"

His eyes dimmed as if someone had pulled the cord on a light.

The bit of information I knew about Bob's family was shorter than his one-liners. "You going home for fall break?" I pressed more gently this time. I wasn't going to barge in on his personal life. He needed to know I respected him, regardless.

Bob finally spoke, shaking his head. "No. No."

I didn't pry and instead belted out a throaty laugh. "Well, that might make two of us." I stopped short, thinking of Sallie Rae and when she'd be back.

He let out a hint of a smile, one of sadness, vulnerability, and pain.

A beat of something like understanding passed between us. I closed my eyes and listened to the birds chirping and the constant little buzzes and noises in the background. Here, on the mountain, life surrounded us—bustling with energy and activity. I raised my head and turned my face to catch the warm rays of the sun. I was in another world. Even the trees joined in softly as the wind rustled their branches, making limbs and leaves dance. The leaves swirled through the air until they settled on the forest floor.

I checked my phone. I had a missed call. Somehow I'd flipped the switch to silent mode. I recognized the number, which I had added to my contacts—Randall's number.

CHAPTER TWENTY

RANDALL HAD LEFT A VOICEMAIL ASKING ME TO CALL. He sounded elated, quipping that he'd finished his last midterm. Since we had put up the flyers, a few calls had come in. A sighting here and there, but none amounted to a real tip when it didn't match up to descriptions of Sallie Rae's car or other details.

"Randall called and left a message," I said. "He's done with exams. I think he wants to come help."

"Any word from Drew?" Bob asked.

I chewed my lip. I'd been focused on Sallie Rae and was relieved now that she was alive and well. But I'd lost sight of Drew. I gulped, and a lump caught in my throat. "You're right. We haven't heard from him."

Clutching my phone, I tapped Randall's number on my recent call list.

He answered on the first ring.

"I got your message."

"Hey, where are you?" Randall said.

"We're here on Snake Mountain."

"You and Bob?"

"Yes, I'm putting you on speakerphone so he can hear. Any word from Drew?" I tapped the speaker icon and got straight to the point.

"Uh ... no."

Bob's eyes met mine. I detected a glint of worry.

"Hey, Randall, do you know what Drew's plans are for fall break?"

"It was confusing, and his plans kept changing."

"What do you mean?"

"His parents were away on business. They were supposed to come back last weekend, but Drew said something came up at the last minute."

"When are they coming back?"

"They were hoping to be back for fall break."

"Do you know how to reach them?"

"Well, let's see. Hold on."

I heard some shuffling of papers and a flurry of activity over the phone. I murmured to Bob, "Hope he finds it." Then I heard a shout.

"Hey, I'm back," Randall said, his breathing quick. "I found it."

"What?"

"Drew's parents—they sent a birthday card to Drew, and it was still in the pile of mail."

"On the kitchen table?" My heartbeat raced.

"Yes. I found it on the envelope—their return address."

I sucked in a breath.

"I'm going to look for him," Randall said. "Drew's my roommate and friend."

I glanced at Bob. He was checking the time and mouthed "yes."

"Randall, we'll swing back to pick you up," I said. "Can you be ready in about an hour and a half?"

"I'll be waiting," he said.

CHAPTER TWENTY-ONE

GOING DOWN THE MOUNTAIN WAS EASIER THAN GOING up. We made good time getting back to Bob's pickup.

My thoughts were racing. *Could this be the first solid lead on Drew?*

Bob cranked up the engine and stomped on the gas pedal. The wheels churned and, with a burst of fuel, took off.

"Do you know Drew well?" I asked.

"Casually."

"Know anything about his parents?"

"They travel a lot. Drew jokes about being an orphan kid."

"No brothers or sisters?"

"He's an only child."

"Sallie Rae was crushed when he went to Europe, and they were apart all summer."

"She couldn't go see him?"

"No. She'd gotten the job at Dr. Parker's office. She didn't have the time or money to travel to Europe."

JANE SUEN

"Drew offer to pay for her trip?"

"Yeah, but her friend Kelly did her a favor passing along the job information, and she couldn't take time off and let her down," I said. "Besides, Sallie Rae was proud of earning her way. She wouldn't accept money from Drew."

"Even if it meant she could be with him?"

"Yes. If you knew Sallie Rae, you'd know. She was torn and almost considered going. But in the end, she didn't."

❧

RANDALL WAS WAITING in front of his place when Bob pulled up. I barely had time to pop open the door before he slid in beside me on the front seat of the pickup.

"Hi, guys," Randall said as he buckled up his seat belt.

I wished I had his energy. After taking two tests, I'd be zonked. But Randall was high, and his excitement was palpable.

"Where to?" Bob asked.

Randall pulled a folded envelope from his pocket and spread it out flat. I typed the address into my map app as he read the it out loud. A blue line appeared instantly.

"Go back on Route 82, then take the second exit and veer right to the next road. Then it's two and a quarter miles up, on the right," I said.

Bob wasted no time taking off.

"Did Sallie Rae mention Drew when she talked to her mother?" Randall asked.

"Nope. It was a short call. I don't think it occurred to Mrs. Landon to ask." I glanced at Randall. "When Sallie Rae called, it caught her by surprise."

"Could she be with Drew?"

I turned back to him, studying his profile, and pondered the question.

"I heard they broke up," I said.

"Where did you hear it from?"

"Erika, her roommate."

Randall snorted.

I twisted around to face him. "You don't believe her?"

"You know she's been after Drew, right?"

My mouth dropped open as a soft "Ooh" escaped.

Bob caught my reaction—not much escaped his attention.

"Sallie Rae and Drew are still together?" I asked. "But why would she spread this rumor?"

"Jealousy. Believe me, it's one-sided. Drew has no interest in Erika." The authoritative tone in Randall's voice was unmistakable.

"I can see why girls like him. I mean, Drew is swoon-worthy handsome, tall, and broad-shouldered. And a real gentleman. He's really nice," I finished lamely.

I sensed Randall was fiercely loyal and a good friend. But sometimes a bit emotional and easily agitated.

CHAPTER TWENTY-TWO

THE SPRAWLING DWELLING WAS A SIGHT FOR THE EYES, rising at the end of a lengthy, winding driveway. It was secluded and surrounded by acres of land. It dwarfed the plain building next to it, which could have been a small barn or shed. I didn't see any animals, but I half-expected a dog to jump out and bark at us.

There were no cars parked in front of the home when Bob pulled up in his truck. It was quiet. Too quiet.

The two guys quickly stepped out of the truck first and waited for me.

"Let's take a look around," Bob said.

We spread out, each headed in a different direction —Randall around the side of house, Bob to the barn or shed building, and I to the front door.

"Is anyone home?" I rang the doorbell, and the sound reverberated and echoed back.

I tried again. "Hello, anyone here?"

It didn't seem like anyone was home. The three of

us met up again and stood on the porch, discussing our next step.

I caught the sound of a vehicle approaching, and I snapped to attention.

A truck appeared, kicking up a cloud of dirt under the wheels. *Who could it be?* I stared, trying to catch sight of the driver and see if anyone else was in the front seat.

"What the heck?" Randall muttered.

The truck was covered in a grimy film, its wheels encrusted with dirt.

"Psst, have you met his parents?" I asked Randall.

He nodded.

The truck screeched to a stop right in front of us. I took a step back as the doors swung open, and two men got out. *These can't be Drew Walker's parents.*

Whoever they were, bashful wasn't a fitting description. The taller man was the driver. The way he walked, he could pass for a ranch hand if he had a cowboy hat. The other guy was older, short and squat, and more muscular. His thick arms were bursting out of his grubby T-shirt sleeves. I sensed the tall guy was the one in charge before a word was exchanged.

"You need to leave," the shorter guy said.

"Is this the Walker residence?" I asked.

"Who's asking?"

"I'm Eve, and this is Bob, and that's Randall. We're Drew's friends," I said, waving my arm in their direction. "We'd like to talk to him and his parents."

"They ain't here." The shorter guy had a smug look on his face. He reached in his pocket and brought out some keys, jingling them before he picked the one he wanted.

I wet my lips. "Look, sir ... "

He didn't offer his name.

I looked down at the keys in his hand and looked up at the door. *Who are these guys with the keys to Drew's parents' home?* I tried again, more carefully this time. "I —we came here looking for Drew."

"He ain't here."

"You live here?" I asked, looking back and forth between the short guy and the taller one, back and forth, meaning I was asking both of them.

The short guy didn't answer. Instead, he jiggled the keys again.

"Do you know when they'll be back?"

"Drew says they're out of town."

I blinked. *Did he say Drew? When did he talk to him?* "You talked to Drew? Where is he?" I yelled. "Who are you guys?"

He glared at me, then spat a stream of dark tobacco juice, aiming for the ground by my foot. "You're tres-passin'. Now get out!"

CHAPTER TWENTY-THREE

THE THREE OF US ABOUT TRIPPED OVER EACH OTHER, running to the pickup. We climbed in and locked the doors.

"Who are they?" I asked.

"They're not Drew's parents," Bob said.

"I've never seen them before," Randall said.

"Let's get out of here." Bob's deep baritone soothed my nerves as he cranked the engine and mashed the gas pedal.

I glanced back at their truck when we passed it and memorized the license plate number. I kept it on the tip of my tongue and repeated it while I dug in my backpack to find my notebook. Flipping open to a blank page, I quickly jotted down the plate number.

"Where are we going?" Randall asked.

"I need to run by Professor Reynolds' office and catch him before he leaves." I glanced at the clock on the dashboard—4:13 p.m. "There won't be time to make another stop before then."

"We'll go with you," Randall said, then he glanced at Bob. "We will, right?"

Bob snorted a good-natured laugh.

I called Professor Reynolds to give him a heads up we were on our way and a quick briefing. I knew he didn't like surprises, and he had a few quirks—who didn't?—and such disruptions wouldn't have been taken favorably. He had been so generous with his time with me at Midway College that I debated whether to impose on him further. But he had jumped in to help with the Sallie Rae case, and this piece of the puzzle would interest him.

We stood outside his office and knocked. "Come in!" he bellowed in his deep voice, projecting authority with ease—born from a natural presence groomed over the years.

Randall gasped softly, skirting carefully around the stacks of papers and books on the floor as we entered Professor Reynolds' office. As usual, his desk was piled with papers, and his corduroy jacket was carelessly tossed over a pile of books on the solitary wooden chair.

Professor Reynolds' way of welcome was to clear the stuff from his chair and beckon me to sit. He didn't apologize for his mess. Bob leaned against the wall and stretched his long legs. Randall stood awkwardly off to the side with his arms crossed.

"Professor Reynolds, thank you for seeing us." I gestured to my right. "Bob Harding. Cassie had invited Bob and me to spend some time with her at Lolly

Beach, and we ended up helping to solve a murder." I turned to my left. "Randall Quinn is Drew Walker's roommate. Drew is Sallie Rae's boyfriend, and we've been trying to find him. We don't know if they are together."

"You called as you were leaving Drew's parents' home?"

"Yes, we didn't see them, but we ran into two unsavory characters," I said.

"His parents have been out of town. Drew had expected them back last weekend, but their plans changed," Randall piped up.

"Maybe these guys were working on the property or keeping an eye out for the Walkers?" Professor Reynolds asked.

I glanced at Bob and Randall, who shook their heads. "I definitely didn't get that impression, either," I said. "They were intimidating, and they didn't want us there, so we left before we had a chance to thoroughly check out the place."

"Eve introduced us, but they didn't say who they were. She wrote down the plate number on the truck they drove," Randall said.

"Can we get someone to check it out?" I asked.

Three pairs of eyes stared expectantly at Professor Reynolds. He frowned and leaned back in his chair, then reached in his desk drawer and pulled out a small, well-worn, leather-bound book. There was a pause as he flipped through the pages. His finger finally rested on an entry, and he looked up.

"There is someone—a private investigator. What's the tag number?"

I flipped open my notepad and read out the number to him as he wrote it down.

"This guy's fast," the professor said, reaching for his phone.

CHAPTER TWENTY-FOUR

The person the professor called answered after a short wait. I gripped the chair's armrest, tensing my muscles. It was a one-sided conversation, but my ears were alert to every word. After Professor Reynolds repeated the tag number, there was a pause. He put his palm over the mouthpiece and whispered, "He's checking now."

I reached in my backpack, took out my pencil, and chomped on it, reverting to my old habit. It was familiar and comforting—the give of the wood as my teeth clamped down, the familiar chalky, graphite-like taste as I bit the lead.

The professor's voice broke in, bringing me to the present. "Send it to me." Then there was a break in the conversation as he went to his computer screen and checked. "Okay, got it. Thanks." There was a hint of a smile as he clicked off, ending the call.

I stopped and whipped the pencil out of my mouth.

He gestured to us to come closer, pointing at his

computer screen. I got up and joined the guys crowded around his desk.

"The tag belongs to Eddie Johnson." He swiveled the screen toward us. "Does this look like the guy who talked to you?"

I squinted. He looked familiar.

"No, he was the taller one who didn't do any talking. It was the other guy who did all the talking," Bob said.

"Uh, his hair—it's longer now and has some curl to it, and he's unshaven. I was so busy talking to the short guy, I didn't pay as much attention to him," I said.

Randall whistled and cursed. "Holy crap, it's him!" he shouted.

"Him, who?" I said.

"Yes, it's him—the guy I saw on Drew's laptop."

We looked at each other in stunned silence.

CHAPTER TWENTY-FIVE

Professor Reynolds whirled back to his computer. The keys made clickity-click sounds as he typed quickly. "I sent a message to get more information."

I sank back down in my chair and repeated the name to myself: Eddie Johnson. *Who is he? A felon with a long criminal record? A petty thief? A murderer? A kidnapper?* My thoughts churned as the link between him and Drew firmed up ... and what about Sallie Rae? *Oh, my gosh. What if she's in trouble?*

Bob rested his hand on my sagging shoulder. I felt the reassuring warmth through the thin cotton of my top and crooked my head, grateful for the comfort of human touch. I was pretty level-headed, but I had my moments, and this was one of them. My insides twisted. I glanced at the clock on the wall—the hour dial had slipped past five o'clock, and the minute hand was at eighteen minutes past. I fixated on the dial as the seconds ticked by. It was agonizingly slow as we waited. At the same time, each passing second meant less time to find them.

The professor's eyes were peeled to his screen, and his fingers hung over the keyboard, waiting. Then the reply came.

I jumped out of my chair and moved to his desk, as did Bob and Randall. Under Eddie Johnson's name, there was a rap sheet a mile long. He'd been in and out of jail since his teens, starting with minor offenses. His early crimes were misdemeanors—petty theft, shoplifting—then he moved on to more serious ones. I skimmed rapidly, looking for the one word that would sink my hopes. I sighed, letting out a long breath when I didn't see murder listed.

"What was Drew doing with his mug shot?" Professor Reynolds asked.

"I don't know. He acted weird when I walked into his room, and he quickly closed his laptop," Randall said.

"And this was when?" Professor Reynolds asked.

"Right before Sallie Rae went missing."

"Do you have an address on his license plate?" I asked.

He scrolled back and searched, pointing to the screen. "It's a local address."

I jotted it down in my notebook.

"Hey, I know that place," Bob said quietly.

"You do?" I turned to him, eyebrows raised.

"It's in a trailer park, on the outskirts of town. I'll take you."

I glanced at the clock; the hand was almost at six.

"Let's go."

WE GOT BACK in Bob's truck. He drove, and I sat in the front with him, squeezed in the middle, with Randall on my right.

"Do we have a plan once we get there?" Randall asked, his voice rising. "I mean, there're two of them against us. What if they have guns?"

"I've got a pair of binoculars in the glove box," Bob said. "We can take turns with them and do a stakeout."

"Great idea." I grinned. "We're not going to barge in there. If Drew's in trouble, we can contact the authorities."

"I still think we should be prepared." Randall stuck his lip out, still fuming.

"Bob's a blackbelt," I said.

"Huh?" Randall stared at me. "Really?"

"Uh, just kidding, but he knows how to fight."

"Guys—you know I'm here, right?" Bob said, pretending to be offended.

"Yeah, yeah." I laughed and relaxed—only for a moment, and then my heartbeat raced.

CHAPTER TWENTY-SIX

THE SLIGHT CHILL IN THE AIR SIGNALED THE ARRIVAL OF the evening. The sun's rays dimmed, and daylight ebbed, retreating into the night. The fluffy clouds darkened with the fading blue sky, and shadows loomed under the trees. The wind stirred, rustling the leaves in the breeze.

We were positioned behind a slight incline overlooking the trailer park. Whoever laid out the homes didn't bother to make them line up straight. Patches of lawn dotted the landscape, some freshly mowed with flowers planted in neat rows, others unkempt, with rusty lawn chairs, plastic toys, metal trash cans, discarded tires, and various junk scattered across the yards.

Bob volunteered for a reconnaissance trip. Eddie's trailer was off to the side. The curtains were drawn, and it was dark inside. We kept Bob in sight as he crept closer and listened for sounds over the hum of electric units. Randall and I took turns keeping watch with our binoculars to alert Bob if we saw Eddie's truck drive up on the narrow road. After scouting around, he climbed back up to join us.

It was evening when Eddie Johnson drove up in his truck, the headlights bouncing on the uneven gravel road. The fading lights strung across the trailer park cast a muted glow, barely lighting up the place.

We watched as the truck pulled up in front of the trailer door, and Eddie got out, walked to the rear, and let down the tailgate. The short guy opened the passenger door and came around the back to join him. They reached for something wrapped in a carpet roll. Each man grabbed one end of it, and they lifted it off the truck and dumped it on the ground. Eddie took the keys out of his pocket, opened the trailer door, and flipped a light switch inside. Soft yellow light spilled out and illuminated the steps. The men hoisted the load and carried it inside, the shorter guy kicking the door shut.

Randall was watching through the binoculars, and he was beside himself. He whispered, trembling with panic. "Shit, I think they've got Drew."

"How can you tell?" I said.

"The thing they were carrying. I saw it move," Randall said emphatically. "I bet they nabbed him when they found him at his parents' house; then they waited until dark to bring him here."

"He's alive?" Bob asked.

"Well, I saw it move. And they'd be stupid to bring a dead body in their house," Randall said, fuming. "If he was dead, they would've dumped him somewhere else."

"Maybe they're waiting for his parents to get back and are holding Drew here for ransom?" I said.

"'Cause they couldn't leave him there," Randall added, finishing my thoughts.

"Exactly," I said. "What's next?"

"Drew needs our help," Bob said quietly.

"How are we going to do it? We can't just walk in and grab him and take him out, can we?" I asked.

"You'd rather sit back and call for help and wait until they get here?"

"Hey, I'm just asking."

"I'm with Bob. I say we go in. If Drew gets hurt, I'm not going to stand by and do nothin'. No telling how long it'll take for the police to get here. What if they can't get a search warrant for the trailer or can't find a judge to sign off on it first? Shit, Drew could be dead if we don't act now," Randall hissed.

"All right, I'm with you guys, but do you have a plan?" I said.

"I'll create a diversion. Draw them out. Then you two go in and extract Drew." Bob reached in his pocket and pulled out a knife. "Randall, take my knife. I've got some rope and tape and other stuff in my backpack. Each of you get something."

This was the most I'd ever heard Bob speak in one breath. I was amazed the man could give orders and take action—at the same time—in a crucial moment.

"I've got pepper spray in my backpack," I said as I ran back to grab it. Randall was hot on my heels, diving in to look for Bob's backpack.

Randall and I quickly gathered the items we needed, and we met up with Bob.

"Ready?" Bob asked.

Randall nodded, and I gave a thumbs-up.

"You guys follow me. Wait till I lure them outside." Bob tightened his belt, pushing his shoulders back. "Okay, let's go get Drew."

CHAPTER TWENTY-SEVEN

THEY SAY THE REAL CHARACTER OF A MAN IS REVEALED when he is faced with hard choices. Would he run toward danger to save someone else? Or instead, run the other way?

The three of us didn't hesitate. We knew what we had to do. Would Eddie Johnson or the short guy have guns? I dialed Professor Reynolds' number. When he didn't answer, I left a long message. I closed my eyes and said a quick prayer for us, then straightened up.

Bob led the way, and Randall and I followed close behind. Bob was familiar with the place, having scouted it. I kept my eyes on the ground, each foot planted firmly as I descended down the incline. We traveled in single file. Bob wheeled around and motioned for Randall and me to keep quiet with one finger up across his lips. We crouched alongside the frame of Eddie's trailer.

In the distance, dogs barked. Someone yelled as a screen door slammed. A baby cried. Music blared out of an open window. Across from Eddie's yard, the light of a TV screen flickered, and the sounds of laughter erupted from a sitcom.

I recognized the truck parked in front of his trailer. Bob moved quickly to the truck and tried the door. He opened it quietly, slid into the driver's seat, and looked for keys. They weren't in the ignition. He unscrewed the panel covering the ignition system and steering column, located two ends of the wire, and hot-wired the truck.

"I'm going to draw them out," Bob said as the engine roared to life. "You guys get ready."

I shoved a thumbs-up sign toward him.

Bob snapped on the seat belt, honked the horn, and turned on the truck's headlights. He pumped the gas pedal, revving the engine. The trailer door flung open, banging against the door frame.

"Hey!" The short guy dashed out, yelling and running toward the truck as Bob started driving away, keeping his speed slow until he could see the guy through his rearview window.

Randall and I stayed low, watching for the other guy, Eddie. He appeared on the steps, then went back into the house, grabbed something in his hand, and also took off running after the truck. I sprinted straight for the door and motioned for Randall to follow.

I spotted a dark object—the carpet rolled up with something inside. I poked it and called out, then heard a muffled sound, so I took the knife from Randall and quickly cut the ropes around the carpet. We had to shove it to the other side of the trailer to make room to unroll it. Randall pushed, and I pulled to unravel the roll. The carpet was heavy, and I was panting and groaning with the exertion. We got it to the point where we could see the legs poking out, and they were tied. I cut them loose, then the arms tied behind the back. We flung the last piece of carpet off the body.

"It's Drew!" Randall yelped, whipping away the duct tape covering his mouth. Drew's eyes blinked as he worked his mouth to speak.

I heard a sound and swiveled to see Eddie's figure looming in the doorway behind Randall. In a split second, he rushed him, throwing a couple of punches so fast that Randall staggered, tripped over Drew's body on the floor, and fell.

I screamed.

Eddie spun around to me, a gun in his hand.

"Drop the knife," he said, raising the gun and pointing it at me.

I froze.

"Do it!" he screamed, brandishing his gun.

I gripped the handle of the knife, feeling the weight of it, thinking it was heavier than it looked. My hand shook.

Eddie's face was flushed, twisted, and contorted in rage, the muscles on his neck corded, straining to pop. He started moving slowly toward me.

I let go of Bob's knife, and it clattered on the floor.

"Kick it to me."

I kept my eyes on the gun and bent my knee, kicking the knife over.

"Now sit down," Eddie barked, waving his gun.

He closed the gap, suddenly grabbed my left foot, and pulled me toward him. He set the gun down and picked up a roll of rope on the floor.

I licked my lips, tasting the salt in the beads of sweat on my skin.

I had a split second to take action before Eddie succeeded in twisting the rope around my ankles and tying them. I took a deep breath, using the momentum to heave and kick him in the face with my free right foot.

Surprised and stunned, he howled and let go of my foot. I pulled my leg in and regrouped. Then I got up, stumbled, and backed up against the wall. I was cornered. In desperation, I slid my fingers into my jeans pocket, probing for my pepper spray. I found it. I whipped it out and wrapped my fingers around the canister to secure my grip. He hesitated briefly. I aimed the spray straight at his eyes, pressing with my thumb to release a stream as he charged, lunging toward me.

Eddie roared in pain like a wounded animal, using his sleeve and a handful of his shirt to wipe his eyes.

I ran around him, heading for the door, but tripped over the edge of the carpet and fell, knocking the spray canister out of my hand. It clattered as it hit the floor and rolled beyond my reach.

Eddie grasped my legs and yanked hard. I cried out as his fingers tightened around my shins. I was caught in a vice grip, unable to free my legs as he clenched them and squeezed. I fought, flailing and screaming, and stretched my arm to reach for my spray but came up short. I moved my other arm, my fingers exploring the floor—until they touched cold steel.

It was the knife—Bob's knife. I felt for the handle and wrapped my hand around it.

I twisted my body around as Eddie rose from the floor, his face a swollen, bloody mess, then raised my arm, gripping the knife in my hand. *Could I kill a man?*

"Drop it!"

I froze again.

Bright lights blasted into the room as blue lights whirled and sirens shrieked outside.

CHAPTER TWENTY-EIGHT

I DREAMT I WAS SINGING AND DANCING IN THE FOREST. Flowers adorned my head, wrists, and ankles. A chorus of chirping birds accompanied me. A doe shyly nudged me, and I reached out to touch her. The forest was my stage, and the creatures my audience. I twirled in my bare feet, doing pliés and leaps into the air. My feet glided and jumped across the forest floor. I curtsied when the dance ended, but as I looked down, I saw snakes slithering around my feet, and the whole ground was crawling with them.

"Eve. Eve!"

Someone called my name, and I felt a hand pressing on my shoulder, gently shaking me. Opening my eyes, I saw Bob bent over me, calling my name again.

"Where ... where am I?" I was groggy, and I didn't recognize the room—plain, white.

"Hey, you're okay, Eve. You're in the hospital," Bob said.

"What happened?"

"They brought you in here after you were attacked by Eddie. Your legs have ugly bruises, and you suffered some minor injuries. But you're going to be fine."

I raised my head and gazed around. I was on a hospital bed. Sitting on a table alongside my bed was a pitcher and a cup with a straw bent at ninety degrees next to it. I licked my dry lips—a funky taste lingered in my mouth.

"Water," I whispered.

Bob picked up the water pitcher and filled the cup. As he held the cup for me, I sucked loudly on the straw, slurping up every last drop.

Finished, I wiped my mouth with the back of my hand and remembered my manners. "Thanks," I said. "Where's Randall? How is he?"

"He's here also. He's got facial lacerations, a busted nose, and hematomas from the punches. He'll be going home today too."

"Good. What about you?"

"I didn't get hurt. The short guy chased me in the truck, but he didn't have a gun."

"What about Eddie?"

"Oh, he's being treated here. But he'll be transferred to the jail."

I scrunched my face, trying to recall what had happened. "How did ... "

Bob smiled. "Professor Reynolds. He called the police after he got your message. You're lucky they got there in time."

"Thank him, please," I muttered.

I pushed my elbows to rise up in my hospital bed.

"And Drew?" I cringed, searching his eyes for an answer.

Bob breathed in and out. "Drew is being checked over. They found him dehydrated and weak. He's been beaten. They're going to keep him for a little longer."

I relaxed, my head sinking back on the pillow. "Do his parents know?"

"The police met them at the airport, and they are with Drew now."

I sighed and closed my eyes, but my mind was restless, and somewhere in there, a niggling thought was jostling my mind—Sallie Rae! My eyes flew open, and I reached out and grasped Bob's arm. "We *have* to talk to him!"

He removed my hand and squeezed it. "We will. Rest up now. The others will be here soon."

CHAPTER TWENTY-NINE

Professor Reynolds came by to see me later. One look at his face told me he was genuinely worried. I think he felt protective and responsible for what happened to me.

I waved him over. "Thank you. You saved me—I mean, us."

He relaxed his frown and cleared his throat. "You guys were the brave ones."

"How's Drew? Have you talked to him?" I asked.

"Not yet, but I've talked to Bob and Randall."

"I'm worried."

"About him?"

I shook my head. "Sallie Rae."

Bob popped his head in the doorway and grinned when he saw us both.

I waved at him to come in.

Randall appeared behind him and walked in as well. "How're you feeling?"

"Better," I said, "And you?"

"Yeah."

"I want to talk to Drew before I leave. You guys want to come with me?"

They replied with a chorus of yeses. Bob led the way to Drew's room down the hall. He knocked and called out before we entered. "You decent?"

He was met with raucous laughter from inside.

"Okay, we're coming in."

Drew was sitting up in bed, his blue-patterned hospital gown tied in the back.

I felt a tap as Randall squeezed past me and marched quickly to his bedside. "Oh, man, it's great to see you."

"Likewise," Drew said, his voice choking when he saw his roommate and then the rest of our group. "Thank you all."

"You're going to be released tomorrow?" I asked, grasping his hand. I shuddered, looking at his bruises and bandaged cuts. "Thank God, you're alive."

Drew's face puckered, lower lip quivering as he held back tears.

I gave him a hug and a squeeze, feeling the tenseness in his muscles. "We were worried about you." I tilted my head toward my teacher. "Have you met Professor Reynolds? If it wasn't for him tracking you down, you wouldn't be here now."

"Thank you," Drew said, tearing up.

"Man, we couldn't get hold of you," Randall said.

"I'm sorry," Drew mumbled between sniffles.

Bob snatched the tissue box from the counter and slid it in front of Drew.

"Tell us what happened," Professor Reynolds urged.

CHAPTER THIRTY

Drew snatched a tissue and dabbed the corners of his eyes. He sighed.

"My parents didn't make it back last Friday. Something unexpected came up, delaying them for a few days. Mom, especially, was worried about her new cat, Rambunctious. She asked me to check up on him. 'Drew, honey, make sure Rambunctious doesn't run out of food and has clean litter.' Hence, I rushed over to their house."

Drew raised up on his elbow and readjusted his pillow. "When I got there, Rambunctious was not a happy camper. He'd gotten into stuff and made a mess. He'd ripped open the cat food bag, and he was still on the hunt for food." Drew snorted, laughing. "Oh, if you ever want to see a pissed-off cat, I have just the one for you. Anyway, I was so focused on the cat; I didn't hear anyone come in." His smile faded.

Randall sucked in a breath.

Drew continued. "They tied me up and locked me in the basement."

"Eddie?" I asked.

"Yeah."

"What about the other guy?"

"He was there."

"Were you hurt?"

"Eddie ... he splashed water on my face and laughed. He roughed me up. Slapped me when I struggled. Tied me up. He made sure I knew who the boss was."

"What's his beef?" Bob asked.

"He wanted something."

"What—money, ransom?" Randall interjected.

He shrugged.

"I'm sorry," I said. "What did your parents tell you?"

"Eddie had come around asking for work. Dad turned him down politely and said he didn't have any work at the moment, but he took Eddie's name and number and said he'd call. I bet Eddie took it as an invitation to 'come back later,'" Drew said, making quotation marks with his fingers.

"The day I barged in your room, I saw you looking at a mug shot—Eddie's. What are you not telling us?" Randall said. It sounded accusatory to me.

Drew shifted in his bed. "A few days after the incident, Dad discovered some damage to his barn and a dead bird inside with its throat cut." He grimaced. "He didn't tell Mom and told me not to say anything to her, 'cause he didn't want to upset her."

"Or scare her," I mumbled.

"Dad was furious. Livid. But he and Mom were

leaving on the trip, and he didn't have time to deal with it." Drew paused. "Said if any harm came to Mom's precious Rambunctious, he'd never hear the end of it. Dad asked me to look into this guy, Eddie."

"So that explains why you were checking on him. He has a rap sheet. Been in and out of trouble. Petty crimes and some heavier shit," Randall said.

I'd been dying to ask him about Sallie Rae. In the excitement and flurry of events, she had escaped our attention. I leaned forward. "Drew, I know you've been through a lot. I'm going to ask a personal question if you don't mind."

He stared at me.

"Sallie Rae. Have you seen her?"

"I ... I haven't talked to her for a few days."

"Her mother reported her missing on Saturday, but Sallie Rae called her on Sunday and said she was okay, but she wasn't coming home yet."

Drew's eyebrows raised, and his eyes widened.

"I don't mean to upset you," I said, reaching around to tuck in a loose corner of his thin hospital blanket. "Why don't you rest for now? We can talk later."

CHAPTER THIRTY-ONE

I CHECKED OUT OF THE HOSPITAL AFTER THE DOCTOR released me, wincing when I bumped the bruises on my leg. I should be grateful my bones weren't broken. Bob dropped off Randall, then he took me home and insisted on helping me walk to the front door. More than anything, I wanted peace and quiet. I hadn't been thrilled about the hospital and was looking forward to my own bed.

"I can take it from here," I said, standing on the threshold, one hand on the front door.

Bob hesitated.

"No, I'm a big girl. Thank you." I threw him a weak smile and closed the door.

I tore off my clothes, walked to the laundry room, and threw them in the washer. Next stop was the bathroom. I turned on the shower, waited for the water to heat up, and stepped in, closing my eyes and standing under the shower for what seemed like an eternity.

I was exhausted, physically and mentally. I went

through the motions of shampooing my hair, scrubbing my skin with soap, and rinsing. It was my daily ritual. Relaxing, comforting, habitual.

Being on autopilot gave me a chance to let my mind wander freely. Flashes of recent events popped up, unbidden. I didn't want to relive every moment. Yet my mind was processing these memories, tucking them in compartments and filing them away for future use.

After my shower, I crashed on the bed and fell into a deep slumber. A faint voice called out to me. I was in a strange place, barren and stark. It was unreal, like I had been transported to another realm. I rotated my body 180 degrees, but everywhere, the landscape was exactly the same. I opened my mouth to holler, releasing the air in my lungs, then ran, desperate to escape, faster and faster. I was on a treadmill, quickly going nowhere.

A persistent ringing finally penetrated my consciousness and woke me up. I thought it was part of my nightmare, this constant ringing. On the side table, my phone lit up, announcing an incoming call. I rolled over in bed and stretched out my arm to retrieve it.

Mrs. Landon's voice blurted out a cheery hello.

"Good morning," I mumbled.

"Err, it's afternoon. Are you okay, Eve?"

"My circadian rhythm is off. What can I do for you?"

"I heard on the radio. You guys rescued Drew at the trailer park."

I straightened up on the bed. "I haven't listened to the radio today."

"Well, it made the news. Good job."

"We all did it together," I said, blushing and thankful she couldn't see my face.

"It answers one question."

"What? That they didn't run off together?"

"That's for sure. It would've been easier if they had."

"What do you mean?"

"Now we're back to square one. I mean—"

"Yes?"

"The mystery deepens. Where's my Sallie Rae?"

"Mrs. Landon, the fall break starts tomorrow. The school will be essentially shut down until classes resume on Monday."

"Five days." Her voice wavered.

"Yes. Look, Mrs. Landon, you can call me anytime. I'm not going home."

"But your mom—"

"She understands."

"I'm sorry to ruin your break."

"Break's not started."

"I've been harder on her than usual lately," Mrs. Landon said.

"Why?"

"She had a tough time this summer, working here. I knew she'd rather be with Drew, and she missed him, but I gave her an ultimatum—stay here and work or don't come back."

I bit my lip. If she had done it to me, I'd be long gone, after a few choice words.

"I was afraid I'd lose her when I put my foot down."

"The more you apply force, the more she'll rebel."

"I've been thinking all this was my fault. I forced her and pushed her away."

You should feel guilty, I thought. *I wouldn't blame Sallie Rae if she left.* Instead, I said, "Mrs. Landon, you need to have this talk with your daughter, not me. All these years, Sallie Rae has been sweet and obedient. But it wasn't good enough for you. She's never met your standards no matter how high she jumped." I was on a roll, and I spelled it out. All. Of. It. "I don't think you'd be satisfied even if Sallie Rae were a saint."

There was a long silence on the other end. Okay, maybe I said too much. But the truth hurt. Knowing Sallie Rae and how much she'd put up with, it *had* to be said. I waited, tapping my fingernails on the back of the phone. How this woman ever birthed a gentle, sweet soul like Sallie Rae was beyond me. She was the one who should beg forgiveness. Maybe Sallie Rae did run away.

"Uh, Mrs. Landon—"

She cut me off, hanging up and ending the call abruptly.

CHAPTER THIRTY-TWO

I CALLED ERIKA, SALLIE RAE'S ROOMMATE.

"Hi, this is Eve."

"Oh." She didn't sound too thrilled to hear from me.

"I just got a call from Mrs. Landon."

"Sallie Rae went home?"

"No. She called her mom on Sunday to let her know she was okay after she heard on the radio the authorities were looking for her. Has she called you?"

"Nope."

"Are you going away for fall break?"

"Packing up now."

"Okay. Keep me posted if you hear anything."

I thanked her and signed off.

My belly chose that moment to growl. I got off the bed, put my slippers on, and walked to the kitchen. I opened the refrigerator, which contained practically nothing. I didn't want to cook and didn't have food to eat. Time to go out for a nice, hot meal.

I SETTLED in my usual spot at the diner. I was what you'd call a regular customer. I didn't need a menu, and they stopped giving me one months ago. The place wasn't far. It was conveniently located off Route 82.

The waitress had thick auburn hair pulled back in a twist. She brought me coffee as soon as I sat.

"Thanks, Pam." I smiled, reaching for the mug, the steam rising over it.

"The usual?" She didn't break out her pad.

"Yes, please."

She walked briskly to the kitchen and hollered my order. In no time at all, she was back with a full plate of fried okra, mac 'n cheese, lima beans, and mashed potatoes.

"Heard about y'all rescuing the guy on the radio," Pam said.

I blushed. "I haven't listened to the radio."

"It's probably the most excitement the trailer court has had." She winked and laughed.

"Are you from around here?" I asked.

"All my life."

"Heard of this Eddie guy?"

Pam leaned toward me and lowered her voice. "Back in the day, when we were in high school ... " She gave a shy smile. "I had a crush on him. So did lots of the girls. He was a sexy bad dude. Irresistible."

"Did you date?"

"I dreamt about him all the time. But no, we didn't.

My daddy said he'd turn out no good." She sighed. "And he was right."

"How did he get mixed up on the wrong side of the law?"

"Once you go down that path, it's hard to change."

I switched topics. "You heard about Sallie Rae on the radio?"

She nodded. "I heard them talk about the girl that went missing. But, didn't she show up?"

"No, here's what she looks like," I said, pulling out my phone to show her the photo.

She leaned in.

"This is Sallie Rae. Do you remember seeing her?"

She paused, scrunching her face. "Come to think of it, she has come in here, maybe once or twice."

I sat up in my chair. "What else do you recall?"

"Well, she's a pretty girl. And she was sweet and polite."

"Was she alone?"

Pam frowned. "I think one time she was, but the other time she wasn't."

My heart thumped in my chest.

"The time she wasn't alone, when was it?"

"Last week."

I enlarged the picture of the couple and thrust the phone in front of her face. "This is Sallie Rae on the left." I pointed to Drew, my fingernails tapping the screen. "Is this the guy you saw her with?"

She shook her head slowly. "It wasn't him."

"Are you sure?"

"Yeah, I'd know it if I saw him again."

CHAPTER THIRTY-THREE

PAM GAVE ME A VAGUE DESCRIPTION OF THE MAN. SHE couldn't remember the details, but she was adamant he was with Sallie Rae at the diner, saying he'd paid cash and left her a big tip.

I sat, holding my fresh, refilled mug, letting my thoughts run free. I wasn't going anywhere with this. It didn't make sense. Why did Sallie Rae disappear and then call her mother to say she was okay? Where was she?

THE NEXT MORNING my phone lit up with Randall's face showing on the incoming call. I smiled, recalling he had inserted his photo. I tapped to answer.

"Hey."

"Drew's home from the hospital. Er, you wanted me to let you know."

I scratched my head. "Oh, right."

"Everything okay?"

"Been thinking about Sallie Rae."

"You want to come over and talk?"

"Yeah, I'll text Bob and see if he wants to meet us."

"See you in a few," Randall said.

As it turned out, Bob showed up about the same time as I did. We parked and marched up the sidewalk. He squeezed my shoulder. I was tensed up, my muscles screaming for a massage. My hand-held back roller would be put to use once I got home.

I knocked on the door.

"Door's open," Randall hollered from inside.

Bob and I walked in. Drew was spread out on the living room couch, a throw pillow under his head, his long legs stretched across the length of the couch, feet hanging over the end.

He gestured to a couple of chairs, which looked just like the ones from the kitchen.

"Please have a seat. Don't mind if I don't get up."

"Not at all." Bob let me pick first, and he took the other chair after I was seated.

Randall was perched on a footstool.

"How are you?" Bob asked.

"The whole hospital thing depresses me."

"Well, you're home now," Randall cheered.

He was like the biggest cheerleader. Pepped up my mood, too.

"Do you mind if I ask a few more questions?" I kept my voice low and soothing.

"Go right ahead."

"Well, I got to thinking about the timeline. You know, Sallie Rae was reported as missing by her mom on Saturday morning." I paused. "When did you last see Sallie Rae?"

Drew closed his eyes and turned his face away from us.

I gave him as much time as he needed.

He gulped. "We met Friday afternoon, after her last class."

"About what time?"

"Oh, I'd say around four or a few minutes after."

"That fits in with our timeline."

"She left the grocery store shortly after three that afternoon," Bob said, affirming what we knew.

"How did she seem?"

"Edgy. I dunno."

"Was she on her way home?"

"She didn't say. We met at our favorite spot off Route 82."

"What did you talk about?" I asked.

He shifted, then he clenched his fist, stretching the skin over the knuckles.

I touched his hand gently.

"I ... I broke up with her," he uttered hoarsely. Drew pressed his back against the couch. A haunted, pained look flickered across his face.

I gasped and realized I wasn't the only one in the room making a sound.

Bob drew in a sharp breath, and he stared at Drew.

Randall stumbled for words, his mouth falling open. "Oh, shit."

"You ... did what?" I stuttered.

CHAPTER THIRTY-FOUR

HE HUNG HIS HEAD. THE MAN LOOKED MISERABLE, AND it wasn't from being in the hospital. My heart skipped a beat, seeing the guilt written all over Drew's face—and regret and pain.

"You haven't talked to her since?"

"Drew left his phone here," Randall piped up.

"I didn't even know Sallie Rae was missing ... until you guys told me," Drew said.

He had a point there. No phone. Tied up by Eddie and his buddy. No communication with Sallie Rae.

I sighed. The room was silent, each of us lost in our own thoughts. Another dead-end. Oh wait, the letter from Sallie Rae—had Drew seen it?

"Hey, Randall, you still have the letter from Sallie Rae?"

He scrunched his brows; then his eyes lit up. "Yes, it's still on the kitchen table." Randall stole a glance at Drew, then looked back at me. I nodded encouragingly.

"I'll be right back," he shouted, sprinting toward the kitchen.

I could hear the sound of mail being tossed, the soft plop of paper landing on top of paper. A triumphant yell told me he'd succeeded. I didn't bother to explain to Drew. He'd find out soon enough. I glanced at Bob. He stayed silent.

Quick steps sounded as Randall bounced back into the living room. He waved the letter and handed it to Drew.

"What's this?" Drew asked.

"It came while you were gone," Randall said. He pointed to the return address.

Drew let out a deep breath; his hand shook as he took it. He didn't open it right away. He stared at the letter, holding it with both hands. "Sallie Rae," he muttered.

"Dude, aren't you going to open it?" Randall waved the letter opener.

Drew looked up, his eyes fixated on the blade. He slowly reached out, took the letter opener from Randall, slit the envelope, and carefully set the blade down.

All eyes were on Drew as he read the letter. It was personal, and we didn't intrude on his privacy. But if it had any helpful information to find Sallie Rae, I was going to make sure to get it out of him.

"What does she say?" Randall blurted out, his voice high pitched.

I was glad he asked. I wanted to know. One look at Bob confirmed he wanted to know, too.

Drew glanced at the letter quickly, reading the first few lines, then placed it on his lap. His eyes misted. "Sallie Rae wrote me a love letter. I broke her heart."

"Do you love her?" I whispered.

His lips parted. I leaned in to catch his words.

CHAPTER THIRTY-FIVE

I KNEW RANDALL WAS IMPATIENT, AND HE COULD ALSO be bold, crass, and rude. Truth be told, he was a breath of honesty and a rare breed. But this time, he even outdid himself.

"You love her, Drew," Randall said, not waiting for his answer. "You need to tell her."

Drew ran his hands through his thick, dark hair. He shook his head. "It's complicated."

"Well, you'd be a fool to let her go," Randall said.

"Things have been strange lately."

"What do you mean?" Randall narrowed his eyes.

"She's different. Moody, testy."

"Do you know why?" Bob asked.

Drew tilted his head. "Sallie Rae's been obsessed ... you know, about finding her father. Her mother said he left before she was born, so she's never met him."

"Is he alive?" I asked.

"She didn't know." Drew hunched his shoulders and scanned our faces. "Last summer, I was in Europe. We were apart for months. Sallie Rae went back home and got a job in a doctor's office. Helped out her friend Kelly."

Bob and I exchanged glances. We had talked to Kelly.

"So, somehow, she got this idea to do a DNA test. When the results came back, she found out she got a match, a high probability. Sallie Rae consulted with a genealogist. She was torn about what to do."

I hung on to every word.

"What did she do?" Randall asked.

"Sallie Rae contacted this guy, and she wrote to him. She didn't want to get her hopes up high—there's still a fraction of probability they aren't related."

"Did she meet him?" I asked.

Drew sighed. "She told me they were meeting for dinner. I offered to come along, but she said no, she wanted to go alone and do this by herself." He paused, shaking his head. "We had an argument. She was bull-headed. Showed a side I'd never seen. And we exchanged more heated words."

I squeezed his hand, offering my support. The letter slid off his thigh, landing on the floor. Randall snatched it up. In doing so, he eyeballed the letter. Drew didn't protest, so Randall read it. His eyes widened when he reached the end. He jumped up suddenly.

"We've got to leave. Right now," he yelped.

Drew snatched the letter back, and I bent my head over his shoulder, relaying it aloud for Bob's benefit. "Sallie Rae wrote she was going to tell her mother. She anticipated it would be difficult. Sallie Rae had insisted on proof and wanted the man who's likely her father to meet with her and her mother—all three of them together. It was the only way to eliminate any doubt in Sallie Rae's mind."

I paused, coming to the end. "She added a P.S. 'The reunion is planned on the first day of fall break at noon. Our favorite place.' That's it," I said.

Randall whipped out his phone and checked the time. "C'mon, we've got an hour and a half." He was raring to go and knelt in front of Drew, staring into his moistened eyes. "You know why she's telling you?"

Drew tilted his head, rubbing the back of his neck as if it were stiff. "Well ... "

"If you love her, you'll go." Randall's voice softened. "She needs you, buddy."

CHAPTER THIRTY-SIX

MAYBE IT WAS RANDALL'S DOING. BUT DREW SNAPPED out of it. I offered to drive, and we piled into my car, Bob and I in the front, the other two in the back seat.

"You know where you're going?" asked Drew.

"I know where I need to go," I said as I revved up the engine, put the gear in drive, and headed to Route 82.

It was a blustery day, partly cloudy, with intermittent rain forecasted after the storm. The wind rattled the trees, shedding their autumn leaves and leaving a carpet of golden yellow, brilliant scarlet, red-orange, and russet leaves on the wet, glistening highway.

My heart was racing, each mile bringing us closer to finding Sallie Rae.

❧

I PULLED off Route 82 and drove up the road, arriving at Snake Mountain. I parked and switched off the ignition. I hadn't asked Drew where his and Sallie Rae's favorite place was—I had figured it out.

"How did you know?" Drew gasped, his widened eyes staring at Snake Mountain and then back at me.

I reached across my seat and pulled my backpack from the passenger-seat floor. My fingers lingered on the zipper tab.

My eyes met Drew's. I paused, pressing my lips together.

I finally disengaged and looked down, pulling on the zipper. I reached inside my backpack, my fingers groping in the side pocket for the object wrapped in cloth. Cradling it in the palm of my hand, I offered it to him.

Drew took it from me and carefully unwrapped the fabric. As the last piece of cloth was peeled back, a grunt from the back seat startled me.

"How in the world?" Randall whistled, jaws slack and eyes peeled on the elegant, dainty ring, the precious stones glittering in the head of the coiled serpent.

"Wh-where did you find this?" Drew stuttered.

"Bob and I, we hiked up the mountain," I said, glancing at Bob. "We stopped to take a break at a clearing, and I found it inside the hut."

"It was where I broke up with Sallie Rae," Drew said, his raspy voice tremoring. He clutched the ring and fingered the smooth curve.

"I'm sorry," I whispered.

"I left before she did." Drew sighed, bending forward, his shoulders in a slump.

"You didn't see her remove the ring?" Bob asked.

Drew shook his head. "I made a quick exit. She probably threw it on the ground."

"It was under the bench," I said, "in the dirt."

Randall interrupted, snapping his fingers. "C'mon, we gotta go!"

I dashed out of the car and grabbed my phone from my backpack. I called Mrs. Landon, but she didn't answer. I tried Deputy Walkins, reached him on the second ring, and gave him a quick update. I left a message for Professor Reynolds.

"Ready?" Bob asked.

They were all standing, waiting for me. I nodded, putting my phone away.

We trudged up Snake Mountain. Drew led the way, walking quickly with brisk, swift steps.

CHAPTER THIRTY-SEVEN

THE FOREST SWALLOWED US UP. IT WAS STRANGELY quiet. Clouds dominated the overcast sky, unwilling to part after the rain. Occasional drops of rain fell from the trees as the branches swayed in the breeze, splattering droplets of cool liquid on my bare arms and landing on my head. It felt refreshing. Overhead, a bird cawed, flapping its wings.

This trek seemed to take longer than the last climb. I kept pace with the others and watched for slithering snakes. Maybe it was the anticipation, the knowing, that stretched and prolonged the time. I raised my eyes, catching sight of Drew and Randall ahead of me on the trail. The sound of Bob's boots crunching the leaves behind me brought a smile to my lips. *He has my back*, I thought, comforted by his presence.

THE BRIGHTNESS above alerted me to the clearing ahead.

Drew waited until we had all caught up with him. "Maybe we shouldn't barge in," he said, stopping and turning around to face us. "What if this doesn't go well?"

"She invited you." Randall pointed his finger, pressing it against Drew's chest. "Man, you're not gonna chicken out."

"We're here with you," I said, touching Drew's arm lightly.

The four of us high-fived each other and crept closer to the edge of the clearing.

"I see movement," Bob said.

"Where?" I whispered.

"Someone's coming out of the hut."

I gasped. "It's Sallie Rae!" We weren't too late. Craning my neck, I strained to see who else was there with her. Another figure emerged, walking slightly to her right. "It's Mrs. Landon."

Bob shifted and moved his arm. His other hand loosened my fingers from his shirtsleeve, releasing my tight grip.

"Sorry," I murmured, taking my eyes off the clearing.

Someone inhaled sharply.

I zeroed in on the door frame of the hut as another person emerged—a tall, fit and handsome, middle-aged man clad in a white T-shirt and dark blue jeans.

Drew chose this moment to walk into the clearing. The three of us scurried behind him.

The man was the first to notice us. Sallie Rae was talking to him, and I saw the look on his face. His arm reached out to her protectively.

"Hey, Drew," Sallie Rae called out, waving her arm. "Eve, Randall, Bob."

The sound of her voice alerted Mrs. Landon. She whirled around and turned toward us, a stunned look plastered across her face.

We dashed across the clearing, Drew in the lead. He stopped short of touching Sallie Rae, hesitating.

Sallie Rae didn't waste a minute. She grinned and threw her arms out to hug Drew, and the three of us, in turn.

"Mom, you know Drew. This is his roommate, Randall. And Eve and Bob."

Mrs. Landon acknowledged us, giving a curt nod.

Sallie Rae turned to the man, smiled shyly, and said, "Uh, y'all, this is my father, Marlon."

CHAPTER THIRTY-EIGHT

DREW WAS THE FIRST TO STRETCH OUT HIS HAND AND shake Marlon's. "Pleased to meet you, sir."

"Been lookin' forward to meetin' you," Marlon said.

"Yes, sir. Me too," Drew said, standing up straighter, every bit respectful and polite.

"I hoped you'd come," Sallie Rae murmured as she moved closer and joined them.

"Long story, but I read your letter today." Drew's brown eyes softened as he gazed deeply into hers.

Sallie Rae tilted her head.

"I—I didn't mean to hurt you. Are you okay?" Drew wrinkled his brow as he leaned in.

She nodded, her face upturned.

"I didn't know all the stuff you were dealing with, and I can't imagine what you were going through. I was frustrated that nothing I was doing was right, and I thought you were pushing me away."

"I was—because I wanted to be alone to figure this

out after meeting Marlon, and I didn't feel like talking or being with anyone. After I disappeared, I spent some quiet time in a little rented hideaway to do some serious thinking. I'm glad you're here now," Sallie Rae said, as a quivering smile widened across her face.

"Will you let me make it up to you?" He stroked her cheeks, tracing her smile.

"You and I have a lot to talk about." She glanced at Marlon, and a light sparked in her eyes. "And we can get to know my father."

Mrs. Landon sniffed, her lips compressed in a thin line.

Randall whooped loudly and clapped Sallie Rae and Drew on their backs. "Way to go, guys."

Turning to Marlon, Randall casually draped an arm around his shoulder. "Now—how is it you left Sallie Rae?"

Marlon threw back his head and ran his fingers through thick, dark hair sprinkled with a few strands of gray. "I never knew nothin' about Sallie Rae. Didn't know her mom was pregnant." He sighed.

"But you left. Why?" Randall asked, his arms now folded across his chest.

A silence fell over us. All eyes stared at Marlon. Tension filled the air.

Marlon shuffled his feet and looked down.

"I was just passing through."

"But—I thought you were married to Mom," Sallie Rae said, a frown furrowing her smooth forehead.

"Her and me ... we weren't married."

Mrs. Landon glared at Marlon, narrowing her eyes, throwing daggers as if looks could kill.

"But—" Sallie Rae's baby blue eyes glistened. She pleaded for an explanation. "I don't understand."

"My best friend was her husband," Marlon said.

CHAPTER THIRTY-NINE

I took a step back. It was like a lightning bolt had hit—smashing the truth that had held everything together.

"Mom, is ... is this true?" Sallie Rae was tearing up now—her voice shaky with disbelief, her world ripped apart.

Mrs. Landon's face turned ashen.

"Let me see if I got this straight," Randall interjected, his eyes scrutinizing Marlon. "Mrs. Landon was married to your best friend. But you got some on the side, too, and created a baby you didn't know about 'cause you were like—how'd you put it?—'just passing through.' Sound about right?"

Marlon nodded, avoiding Randall's gaze.

"You're the baby daddy?" Randall asked.

When Marlon didn't answer, Sallie Rae spoke up. "According to the DNA test."

Mrs. Landon flinched. "What DNA test?" she exclaimed.

"Mom, you know I love you." Sallie Rae gazed at her mother and heaved a sigh. "I've wondered about the father I've never known, but you wouldn't talk about him. So, I did a DNA test and got a match with someone who shared over ninety-nine percent of my DNA. I connected with Marlon, and that's how I found my father."

Gnarled fingers curled and tightened their grip on Sallie Rae as Mrs. Landon yelled, "Let's go. We don't need to hear this crap."

Sallie Rae pulled away, jerking her arm free. "No. *I need* to hear this."

"Wait, what I don't understand is this"—heads swiveled, turning to Randall as he pressed—"did your husband know, Mrs. Landon?"

"It's none of your damned business!" she shouted as her nostrils flared and she seethed with fury. Her eyes dissected him with cold sharpness.

They faced each other, Randall meeting her eyes.

Marlon cleared his throat. "Her husband …"

I stared at Marlon as he continued. "Mr. Landon … well, he er … caught us … me and his wife together."

Sallie Rae gasped and sucked in a breath, covering her mouth with her hand.

"Said he'd kill me if he ever saw me again," Marlon whispered, hunching his shoulders, slouching.

"Shit, that's why you left." Randall blew a long whistle.

"Shut up! Shush your mouth," Mrs. Landon said shrilly, rushing at Marlon with her arms raised and fists pumped.

Bob stepped up quietly and put his strong arms around her, holding her back gently.

Mrs. Landon struggled, her arms flailing. "You ... you piece of shit." Wrenching free, she lurched toward Marlon.

Marlon stood his ground, but his shoulders sagged. The years of living lined his face.

"I didn't know," he said in a weary, monotone voice as he shook his head. He sobbed, his voice giving way to a heart-wrenching cry. "I didn't know nothin' about Sallie Rae."

"After *all* I've done for you," Mrs. Landon screamed, shaking violently, froth oozing from the corners of her lips.

He looked up and stared at her, blinking. "I don't understand—what *did* you do?"

She laughed, long and hard. Her eyes drilled into his.

He frowned, a blank look on his face.

Catching her breath, she started up again between heaves and coughs, letting out a scary, chilling cackle.

Marlon grabbed her arms roughly and jerked her, speaking through gritted teeth. "Tell. Me. What. You. Did." He leaned in closer as blood rushed to his face.

She smirked, her lips curling in an evil grin. "I took care of your best friend. Put him six feet under."

His eyes bulged in horror.

"I made sure he'd never hurt you." Mrs. Landon paused to catch her breath and sneered, hurling her words slowly. "But you, my darlin'—you *never* came back to me."

CHAPTER FORTY

HER WORDS LACED WITH VENOM, MRS. LANDON SPAT, aiming at Marlon. I watched the drool dribbling down his cheeks as he wiped it with the back of his hand.

Sallie Rae took a step toward him, hand outstretched.

Mrs. Landon rushed her, locking her arms around her, growling, "You're coming with me."

Sallie Rae teetered but stood her ground and wouldn't budge.

Everything happened in a whirlwind.

In desperation, Mrs. Landon seized her hand and pulled, pleading, "We've got to go."

"No, Mom, not this time." Sallie Rae shrugged her off.

Enraged, Mrs. Landon screamed, "You ungrateful bitch. After everything—everything I did for you."

Drew darted toward them, pushing himself in between the two women. As Mrs. Landon swung at him, he tried to jerk his head back, but her slap hit his cheek hard, leaving red marks.

Sallie Rae uttered a high-pitched scream.

I stood transfixed in stunned silence.

The sudden snap of twigs and crunching of leaves brought Deputy Walkins and another uniformed officer crashing into view as they sprinted into the clearing.

Mrs. Landon's eyes widened, her face turned pale, her feet rooted to the spot.

Drew caught her arm. Snapping into action, Mrs. Landon pushed him away and tore off, heading to the opposite side of the clearing, into the forest up the mountain.

Running up, Deputy Walkins gestured for us to stay put, shouting, "We'll go after her."

Wordlessly, we eyed each other and nodded in agreement, hesitating briefly before taking off after the officers as they chased Mrs. Landon, and the forest swallowed us, too.

Ahead, a shrill, terrifying scream pierced the air.

I shivered, putting a hand over my heart as a chill ran down my spine. I slowed down, bumping into Bob. Our eyes locked for a second. The others ran past us and were already out of sight. I sensed something was very wrong. My knees felt weak, and I trembled. He took hold of my hand, gently pulling me. I shuffled my feet and took a step, then quickened the pace, with Bob beside me.

We stopped suddenly, coming upon the rest of the group.

Deputy Walkins, the other man in uniform, and Randall were standing at the edge of the steep side of a ledge, looking down. Sallie Rae was bent over, wailing and rocking back and forth. Drew was beside her while Marlon stood close by.

It had been Mrs. Landon's bloodcurdling scream we heard as she made her horrific descent down the deep ravine—plunging to her death.

CHAPTER FORTY-ONE

SALLIE RAE WAS CRYING UNCONTROLLABLY, HER CHEST and shoulders heaving. She kneeled on the edge of the precipice. Drew had dropped on bended knees, wrapping his arms around her to console her.

Mrs. Landon was no longer moving. I squinted to make out her still body, sprawled out and twisted on the rocks below.

I was in shock, no use to anyone. I couldn't find the voice or the words to speak. Bob was silent, too, his face grim. I glanced at Randall, the most fearless, vocal person among us. But for once, he was mute as well— his jaw slack, his mouth open and silent, swaying slightly where he stood.

Deputy Walkins was calling it in as he walked away. *He's seen it before*, I thought, *so death doesn't have the same effect on him as the rest of us. Or maybe he's better at hiding it.*

Marlon had walked off and leaned against the

rough bark of an ancient oak tree. A lone figure. I wondered if he'd ever loved Mrs. Landon or regretted betraying his best friend. What now? Would he come back and stay in Sallie Rae's life?

CHAPTER FORTY-TWO

I RETURNED HOME TO MY MOTHER LATER IN THE evening. I had four more days of fall break left before school started again.

She welcomed me in her arms as she'd always done, but this time, I held on and hugged her long and tight before releasing the embrace. Even then, I didn't want to let her go.

"I love you so much, Mom," I said, holding back the tears.

"I know, baby," she whispered softly. "I love you, too."

She smiled—the beautiful smile I'd loved ever since I could remember.

EPILOGUE

THE SHERIFF EXHUMED THE BODY OF MR. LANDON. HE was buried under the dirt, in the crawlspace of the house where Mrs. Landon lived. He had died on the spot, the back of his skull fractured in multiple places. His death was ruled a homicide.

All these years, Sallie Rae had never seen this dark space under the floorboards where pipes and ductwork ran in the dark bowels of their home. Her mother had made sure of it.

❦

MRS. LANDON WAS BURIED in the cemetery. The only testament to her life was a tiny headstone with her name and dates of birth and death. Grass and weeds proliferated throughout the unkempt grounds and eventually found their way to the new grave. Rain and mud mixed and splashed on the headstone, the dirt obscuring the carved name.

Sallie Rae stood in front of the headstone, her slight figure still. One hand reached in her jeans pocket and pulled out a crumpled piece of paper. Her lips moved as she read a familiar passage—"Forgive me, Father, for I have sinned"—then folded the paper and placed it back in her pocket.

As for Eddie Johnson and his partner in crime, they got into more trouble when Drew's parents, Mr. and Mrs. Walker, arrived back in town and identified them as the two guys who had come looking for work but got pissed off when the Walkers rejected them. Later, they'd come back to the property after the owners left with robbery on their minds, but they got greedy when they saw an opportunity to kidnap Drew for a bigger prize, a huge ransom. This time, though, they wouldn't be getting out of jail any time soon.

It was spring. The colorful wildflowers poked their heads through the shoots of green grass. Butterflies fluttered among the flowers. Birds chirped in the distance. Stately trees rose high above, their branches and new leaves waving in the gentle breeze and casting patterns on the ground below.

Overhead, the sun rose high in the crisp, blue sky, warming the earth and bringing renewed life in the forest.

Gathered in front of the hut where Sallie Rae and Drew had first professed their love were Mr. and Mrs. Walker, Eve, Bob, Randall, Kelly and her mom, Professor Reynolds, Deputy Chat Walkins, and other friends and relatives.

Rocks outlined the pathway strewn with lovely flower petals.

The music started softly, then filled the air, rejoicing for all to hear, including the creatures in the forest.

Sallie Rae walked down the makeshift aisle in a white lace bridal dress, on the arm of her father—looking radiant and turning heads. A wreath of pretty wildflowers adorned her head.

The pastor asked, "Who gives this woman to be married?", and Marlon responded, "I do."

Sallie Rae turned to face Drew Walker, splendid in his matching white tux, a single white flower boutonnière pinned to his lapel. Wordlessly, he reached out and clasped her soft hands in his large, strong hands.

They said their "I dos," exchanged rings and pledges, and the pastor pronounced them husband and wife. Sallie Rae raised her eyes adoringly to her new husband. Drew smiled as he bent his head and whispered in her ear, "Forever, my darling."

BOOKS BY JANE SUEN

Children of the Future

EVE SAWYER MYSTERIES

Murder Creek

Murder at Lolly Beach

Murder off Route 82

FLOWERS IN DECEMBER TRILOGY

Flowers in December

Coming Home

Second Chance

ALTERATIONS TRILOGY

Alterations

Game Changer

Primal Will

SHORT STORIES

Beginnings and Endings: A Selection of Short Stories

ABOUT THE AUTHOR

Jane Suen is an award-winning author who writes mysteries, sci-fi thrillers, short stories, contemporary romance, and crime fiction.

While driving through Alabama on a hot summer afternoon, she saw a "Murder Creek" road sign which inspired her first book in the Eve Sawyer Mystery series. *Murder off Route 82* is her third book in the series.

Made in the USA
Las Vegas, NV
08 December 2021

36548791R00100